Hello!

Horses were always something that I admired from a distance. To be honest, they scared me. They were so big and had big teeth and big hooves, and...yes, I know it sounds silly, but I always figured horses were out to get me.

I had a lot to learn.

I started with a horse barn near my house where the owners were very patient and kind to me; just like they would be with a skittish horse. I learned how to approach a horse, how to make friends, and, eventually, how to ride. It wasn't scary at all. It was like flying.

In this book, David already knows about horses, but he has a lot to learn about responsibility. That's something that most of us struggle with while we're growing up. If you are going to work with animals, you have to be responsible and kind and willing to try new things. It is always worth the effort.

Laurie Halse Anderson

VET
VOLUNTEERS

TRICKSTER

LAURIE HALSE ANDERSON

SCHOLASTIC INC.
New York Toronto London Auckland Sydney
Mexico City New Delhi Hong Kong Buenos Aires

ACKNOWLEDGMENTS

Thanks to Kimberley Michels, D.V.M., and Judith Tamas, D.V.M.
Special thanks to Lynn Willoughby and Glen Michalak of
the Delaware Valley College Equestrian Center of Doylestown,
Pennsylvania, who run an amazing barn.

ISBN-13: 978-0-545-15301-0
ISBN-10: 0-545-15301-8

12 11 10 9 8 7 6 5 4 3 2 1   9 10 11 12 13 14/0

Printed in the U.S.A.   40

First Scholastic printing, January 2009

For my husband, Greg, who makes me laugh

Chapter One

· · · · · · · · · · · · ·

"One waiting room—totally swept," I announce, parking the broom against the wall of the clinic. "Can we go now?"

Brenna Lake turns around at the front door. "Duh, no, David. We can't go until Mr. Quinn calls." She sprays window cleaner on the messy nose prints left by a Saint Bernard. "Keep sweeping," she orders. "I can see dog hair everywhere."

"What are you talking about?" I ask. "I did a perfect job."

"Yeah, right," Brenna says.

We're on cleaning duty today at Dr. Mac's Place, the veterinary clinic across the street from my house. I always knew I'd end up working here. I'm close by, I'm great with animals, and people love me. It took a few years of pestering Dr. Mac, the vet, but she finally caved in.

There are five volunteers: Brenna, Zoe, Sunita, Maggie, and me. Dr. Mac—also known as Dr. J.J. MacKenzie, Maggie and Zoe's grandmother— brought us together a couple of months ago. The clinic was overrun with sick puppies, and she was desperate. We've been regulars ever since.

We help her with all kinds of cases—real emergency room stuff like surgery and day-to-day things like checkups and shots. The medical details are cool, but sweeping floors is the pits. I try not to clean too much. It's bad for my health.

A few more minutes and we are out of here. Today we're taking a road trip.

Brenna sprays the next pane of glass. "I don't know why you're so excited. All we're going to do at Quinn's Stables is shovel manure and bounce along on old horses. What's the big deal?"

"What's the big deal?" I stare at her. Did she really say that? "We're going to be with horses.

That's the big deal! We're going to ride, and groom, and—and—everything!"

My broom falls to the floor with a bang, and Sunita looks up from the receptionist's desk. She's been entering addresses into Dr. Mac's computer. Sunita is the quietest of all of us. She's probably the smartest, too.

"Brenna's teasing you, David," Sunita says. "I think she's as excited as you are."

"Am not," Brenna answers.

"How can you not be excited about riding a horse?" I ask.

"Look, I've ridden before," Brenna says, rubbing the window harder. "It was the most boring half hour of my life."

Brenna is one of those natural kind of girls: old jeans, work boots, save the whales, that kind of stuff. She was the only one who wasn't totally psyched when Dr. Mac told us we'd be helping out at Quinn's Stables for a few weeks. I'll fix that.

"You had a slowpoke, that was the problem," I tell her. "You need a good horse. Mr. Quinn has tons of them. But you can't ride the quarter horse, the one he's picking up in Maryland today. He's all mine."

"The horse cost a quarter?" Brenna teases.

"No—it's a kind of breed. Quarter horses are strong and fast. You've probably seen them on TV. They use them in rodeos for roping and barrel racing. Has to be a smart horse to do that."

"Mr. Quinn won't let you ride a fast, expensive horse," Brenna scoffs. "Not with your history."

"What history?" Sunita asks.

"Didn't you hear what he did?" Brenna puts down the window cleaner and paper towels. "It was in the newspaper last year. David was riding with a bunch of people at Quinn's Stables and took off from the group. It took half the police force to find him."

"That was you?" Sunita asks. "No—even you wouldn't do something like that."

It was a little more complicated than Brenna makes it sound. It happened at the end of fourth grade. Fourth grade stank. I wish I could sweep up the whole year and throw it in the trash. My dad left when I was in fourth grade.

Dad was the one who taught me how to ride. He went to high school with Mr. Quinn, and they had been good friends ever since. Dad had me up on a horse before I learned to walk. Riding was our thing to do together.

I had been thinking about Dad during that famous ride, the one that got me in trouble. He and Mom had separated a few months earlier. He kept promising to visit me, but he hardly ever made it. He promised lots of things that never happened.

Mom was the one who took me to Quinn's that day. She knew how bummed out I was. The split was hard on her, too. I wasn't planning on getting in trouble. I must have lost track of what I was doing. I was just thinking about all the things I wanted to tell Dad, and the next thing I knew, my group had vanished. It really wasn't my fault that they left me behind like that. I tried a couple of shortcuts, but they didn't work like I thought they would. We ended up at the mall, of all places. I couldn't do anything right that day.

When Mr. Quinn arrived with the police, he didn't want to hear my side of the story. I should have paid attention, blah, blah. I didn't listen, blah, blah. I wasn't responsible, blah, blah, blah. And that was the end of horse riding for David Hutchinson.

Until today.

Dr. Mac said the magic words, and Mr. Quinn is giving me another chance.

I really want to make a good impression. The stable is shorthanded because it's final exam time at the high school. This is my chance. If Mr. Quinn sees how hard I can work, he might let me ride there again. That would rock.

Brenna starts on the window next to the front door. "If you don't sweep the floor properly, the only thing you'll be riding is that broom."

"That's so funny, I forgot to laugh."

I sweep the fur balls behind the potted plant. No one will see them there.

"Is it safe to come out?" a voice calls from the kitchen.

Zoe peeks through the door that connects the clinic to Dr. Mac's house. "Is that rat gone?" she asks.

Zoe's a little high-strung, but she's cool. She's hanging here for a while so her mom can move to Hollywood. Her parents are divorced, and she never sees her dad. I can relate to that. Zoe was raised in New York City—excuse me, Manhattan—and living here has been something of a shock for her. Like when a ferret came in earlier, she freaked.

"A ferret is not a rat. It's not even a rodent,"

Sunita explains with a sigh. "Ferrets are related to weasels. Relax, Zoe."

"It has little beady eyes," Zoe says. "I hate those." She eases into the room and closes the door behind her. "Your mom called again, David. That's the fourth time. You really should call her back."

"She probably wants me to take out the trash," I say. "I'll call her later. Hey, Zoe, what do you get when you cross a horse with the house next door?"

She rolls her eyes. "I don't know, David, what?"

"A nei-ei-ghbor!"

"How funny. Did you think that up by yourself?"

The door to the Doolittle examination room swings open.

"The rat! Yikes!" Zoe dashes back into the house just as her cousin Maggie walks out. Close behind Maggie is a college-age guy named Erik holding Rascal-the-ferret's carry cage. Dr. Mac brings up the rear and motions for the owner to go to the receptionist's desk.

"How's Rascal?" I ask.

"He'll make it," Dr. Mac answers. "No broken bones. No internal bleeding. He is one frightened ferret, though. That was quite a fall he took. It's a good thing he landed on a hammock."

Maggie peeks in the cage. "Don't be such a knucklehead," she cautions the ferret. "Next time you'll really get hurt."

"He went right through the screen window," Erik explains as he writes out a check. "He just flew. Sometimes I think he has more energy than brains. What am I supposed to do—keep the windows closed all the time?"

Dr. Mac takes the check from him and hands him a brochure.

"This will give you some tips on how to make your apartment safer. Make sure there are no openings around the pipes under your sink, or he could squeeze in and get trapped in the wall. Don't let him chew on rubber toys, because rubber bits can block his intestines. And he needs a collar with an identification tag and bell, too. That way you won't accidentally step on him."

"Sounds like work," Erik says as he folds the brochure and sticks it in his pocket.

"It's worth it," Dr. Mac assures him.

As Rascal and Erik walk out the door, Dr. Mac

glances at the clock. It's almost four. "Where's Lucas? It's a long drive to Maryland and back, but knowing him, he started before dawn."

"He's probably at the stables wondering where we are," I suggest.

"No way," Maggie says. "You know Mr. Quinn. He's not the kind of guy to stand around waiting for anything. He said he'd call when he got back."

"We'll be patient a little longer," Dr. Mac says as she comes out from behind the counter. "I imagine you're excited about riding again, David."

"Don't get him started," Brenna warns.

I have to grin. "Excited? Try excited times a million! Thanks, Dr. Mac—you know, for talking to Mr. Quinn for me."

Dr. Mac rolls down the sleeves of her shirt and buttons the cuffs. "He didn't take too much convincing. He told me you were one of the best young riders he had ever seen. I hear that you can even ride bareback."

He told her that? "A little. Mr. Quinn taught me. He was teaching me how to jump, too, when I, uh, took that little side trip."

"That's in the past," Dr. Mac says firmly. "Use

your head, be responsible, and Mr. Quinn will be glad to have you around."

Brenna squints and peers out the front window. "Excuse me, Dr. Mac?" she says.

"What, Brenna?" Dr. Mac answers.

"Does Mr. Quinn drive a blue pickup truck with a big dent in the side?"

"A blue truck, yes. But I don't recall a dent."

Brenna points toward the parking lot. "Then someone else just pulled in towing a horse trailer."

I race to the door. "It looks like they were in an accident!"

The truck and horse trailer are a mess. There is a long crease running down the side of the truck and along the side of the shiny silver horse trailer. The small glass window on one side of the trailer is smashed to bits, and the fender over the wheel is just about flattened.

I open the door and run outside. Mr. Quinn is already out of his truck. He looks worried.

The horse in the trailer neighs, a high-pitched scream for help. It sounds freaked out, or hurt, or both. Loud bangs rattle the trailer. The horse is kicking the walls of the trailer—hard.

"Get the doc!" Mr. Quinn shouts.

Chapter Two

. . . .

We got hit on the turnpike," Lucas Quinn explains to Dr. Mac. "A car swerved, clipped the side of my truck, and got the trailer, too. Darn fool took off. Didn't stick around to see what happened."

"At least the trailer didn't flip over," Dr. Mac says.

"It leaned pretty hard, though. Knocked the horse around."

We hear more loud bangs from inside the trailer. The horse sounds like he's about to burst through the walls. He's whinnying loudly.

"We have to get him out," Dr. Mac says. "He's

panicking. Did you unload him after the accident?"

Mr. Quinn shakes his head. "No, I checked and he seemed fine. I wanted to take him straight home, but then he started to tear it up in there. So I decided to come straight here. He's going to need a sedative. You'd better take a look at him."

"I bet he feels trapped," I say. Both adults turn and look at me. "He might be afraid something else is going to hit him, the way the car did."

BANG! BANG! I hope the walls of that trailer are stronger than they look.

Dr. Mac points to the far side of the house. "Back the trailer up to the gate over there," she says. "We'll unload him into the backyard, where it's fenced. He'll feel better if he can walk on grass instead of the driveway."

Mr. Quinn gets in the truck and carefully maneuvers the trailer backward. It rocks back and forth as the horse shifts nervously, snorting and stamping his hooves. When the end of the trailer is up against the gate, Mr. Quinn cuts the engine and gets out of the truck again.

Dr. Mac glances at the five of us. "You all go

through the house and wait on the deck. Horses are unpredictable, and I don't want you too close. If he's spooked or in a lot of pain, he may lash out with his hooves and cause some real damage."

"You mean we can't watch?" Brenna asks.

"You can watch, but you have to stay on the deck."

By the time we sprint through the house to the deck, Dr. Mac and Mr. Quinn are in the backyard. Dr. Mac's cat, Socrates, joins us to watch the show. He climbs onto the wicker rocking chair near Sunita.

"I've untied his halter from the ropes in the trailer," Mr. Quinn tells Dr. Mac. "As soon as we open the back gate, he's free to come out."

"What do you think the horse will do?" Sunita whispers to me.

"He's going to come out of there like he was shot from a cannon," I reply.

"Let's do it," Dr. Mac says.

Mr. Quinn unlocks the back gate, lowers the loading ramp, then quickly gets out of the way.

The scared horse stops stomping and whinnying for a second, then he cautiously backs out of the trailer. As soon as his hooves touch the grass, he twists in the air and gallops at full speed to the end of the yard—*awesome!*

His coat is chestnut, a rich brown color, and his mane looks like someone combed fudge through it. Powerful leg muscles ripple under his shiny coat as he runs, and his black hooves shine in the sun.

I really want to shout at the top of my lungs. This is the most amazing horse I have ever seen! But I bite the inside of my mouth to keep quiet. No sense making the doc and Mr. Quinn angry at me. "I'm going to ride that horse," I vow under my breath.

"What did you say?" Maggie asks.

I shake my head. "Nothing."

When the horse reaches the fence at the end of the yard, he wheels around and gallops toward us, his eyes wide with fear, his ears pinned back. He feels threatened. His gait is a little awkward. One of his hind legs must be bothering him.

The horse runs another lap, then slows down. His eyes relax. His ears come back to their normal, upright position. He's feeling more comfortable.

Dr. Mac speaks softly. "David, go inside and bring out a big bucket of water. He needs a drink."

"Out of the way, out of the way," I tell the girls as I make my way to the sliding glass door. "Horse needs some water."

Once inside, I cut through the kitchen to the clinic and grab a bucket out of the supply closet. I don't want to miss a thing. I fill the bucket to the brim, then speed out the door again.

"Hey!" Zoe complains, as water from the bucket sloshes on her sneakers.

"Hay is for horses," I say, pausing at the top of the steps.

"Shhhh!" warns Dr. Mac.

The horse is standing in the middle of the yard, breathing hard. I can see the sweat on his chest. His eyes and ears sweep across the yard, like he's expecting something else to come along and scare him.

"Bring the water, David," Mr. Quinn says, keeping his voice calm. "He's settling down nicely."

Slowly I walk down the steps. As I get to the bottom, the horse walks straight toward me.

"Don't move," Mr. Quinn tells me. If I hand the bucket to Mr. Quinn, it might startle the horse.

The horse does have a limp. It looks like it hurts him to put his full weight on his hind right foot. As he gets closer, I can see a dark red stream of blood and a cut about two inches long over his right hock.

"What's his name?" I whisper.

"Trickster," Mr. Quinn answers.

Trickster whinnies. The high-pitched sound makes the hair on the back of my neck stand up, like I just touched an electric wire. He stops in front of me, his nostrils flaring, trying to smell me.

I shift the bucket to my left arm and hold out my right hand.

"Hi, Trickster. I'm David."

Chapter Three

. . . .

Trickster stretches his neck. His eyes are warm and friendly. The short hairs of his muzzle tickle as he moves his nose over my hand and up my arm to pick up my scent. I can smell him. Man, it is so good to smell a horse again! For a second, it reminds me of how Dad and I smelled after we came home from the barn. But Dad's not here. It's just me and this magnificent horse.

"Want some water?" I ask, taking the last step toward him.

He looks me straight in the eye. Trickster is smart—I can see that right away. His eyes twinkle for an instant, then he plunges his muzzle

into the bucket. A wave of water soaks my shoes.
I bet he did that on purpose.

He raises his muzzle out of the bucket, shakes
his head once, and his long forelock flops over
his eyes. I set the bucket on the ground and
brush the hair to the center of his forehead. He
shakes his head again so it flops back over his
eyes. He likes his bangs in his eyes, just like me. I
wonder if his mother ever gave him a hard time
about getting a haircut.

"You goofball," I say. He looks totally relaxed
now. His ears are straight up, and he is breathing
slower. His eyes scan the back of the house, taking in the clinic, the girls on the deck, and the
fence line, but he doesn't seem frightened.

Dr. Mac steps closer to Trickster so she can
check him out. "Tell me about him," she says to
Mr. Quinn.

"He's a chestnut gelding," Mr. Quinn says.

A gelding is a male horse that has been neu-
tered to prevent him from fathering any foals.
Dad told me that.

"Five years old, fifteen hands high," he replies,
attaching a lead rope to Trickster's halter.

The height of horses is measured in hands.
One hand equals four inches. Fifteen hands

means that he is sixty inches tall at the withers, where his neck meets his back.

"His previous owners described him as a smart horse, very playful. That's why they named him Trickster. I don't think they appreciated how fast he's going to be. I got a good deal on him."

"OK, buddy, can I examine you now?" Dr. Mac asks as she pats Trickster's strong jaw. "Stay right there, David. He seems to like you."

Dr. Mac uses her stethoscope to listen to Trickster's lungs and heart. "Heart rate is forty-five beats per minute. Respiratory is thirty. A little high, but not scary. I'd say he's still nervous about being hit in the trailer. Did he eat this morning?"

"A grain mix and hay. He doesn't need a special diet. Good thing, too. I already have enough fussy eaters for one barn."

Dr. Mac murmurs to Trickster as she runs her hands over his back, feeling for swelling. He's fine until she gets close to the cut over his right hock. Suddenly, his skin quivers and he snorts hard.

"That's sore, isn't it?" Dr. Mac asks him. She presses gently around the edges of the cut. "He's bruised here. I can already feel the swelling. The cut isn't anything to worry about. We'll treat it with an antiseptic spray, and it will heal on its own."

"Do you think he injured the hip bone?" Mr. Quinn asks.

"Let me feel the leg first." Dr. Mac goes down on one knee and runs her hands down the lower part of Trickster's leg. I hope it's not anything serious. I can already imagine what it will feel like to ride him.

"I want to see him walk," Dr. Mac says as she stands up. "David, take the lead rope and walk him away from us. Slowly, now."

Mr. Quinn puts his big hand on mine as I reach for the lead rope. "She said slowly," he says, giving me a serious look.

"Yes, sir," I answer. I'm going to do exactly what I'm told around this horse, especially when Mr. Quinn is watching.

"Come on," I tell Trickster as we walk away from the house. I walk on his left side by his head. The only sounds in the yard are the soft steps of Trickster's hooves on the grass. It feels so great to be next to a horse again.

"OK, bring him back," Dr. Mac calls.

When I stop, Trickster rubs his jaw against

my hair. "Cut it out," I laugh. We make a wide circle and head back. I look over my shoulder at Trickster's hind legs. He's still limping.

"What do you think?" I ask Dr. Mac as we arrive back.

"I'm pretty sure he hasn't fractured anything, but I want to take some X rays to make sure. I'll be right back. Brenna, I need you to help me carry some things."

Dr. Mac returns from the clinic carrying a portable X-ray machine. The X-ray machine is the size of a toaster oven, with a long electrical cord that she plugs into an outlet on the deck.

Brenna brings out a box and sets it down on the deck. Dr. Mac pulls a heavy apron out of the box and hands it to Mr. Quinn.

"Here's your apron, Lucas."

"What does he need that for?" I ask.

"The apron is lined with lead," Dr. Mac says. "Lucas is going to help me with the X rays. This will block the radiation from his body. Or mine." She ties on a lead apron over her jeans.

"I can help," I say.

Dr. Mac pauses briefly. I hope she's not afraid I'll screw up. "I'll do whatever you say," I add.

"All right," she answers. "You'll need to put on an apron, too."

Dr. Mac holds Trickster's rope while I wrestle with the apron. It is way heavier than it looks. Once it's on, I take the rope back. "Don't laugh at me," I tell Trickster under my breath.

Trickster flares his nostrils and snorts once, blowing my bangs into my eyes.

Mr. Quinn slips on giant mittens that go all the way up to his elbow. "These are lined with lead, too," he explains to me.

Dr. Mac takes a thin metal case the size of a big book and slides it into a slightly bigger wooden box. "The X-ray film is in here," she says, handing the box to Mr. Quinn. "I want you to hold it by the edges and place it right behind Trickster's sore hock."

Mr. Quinn pats Trickster's rump to let the horse know he's there—horses do not like surprises. Then he bends over and holds the X-ray box behind the sore joint in Trickster's back leg. "Is this where you want it?" he asks Dr. Mac.

"Perfect," Dr. Mac says as she picks up the

X-ray machine. "Stay still." She aims the lens at the hock and pushes a button. The machine beeps once.

"Done," Dr. Mac says. She takes out the first X-ray film and puts another in the box. "Different angle this time," she says as she and Mr. Quinn move around.

Trickster twists his head around to see what's going on.

"Relax," I tell him. "They're just taking pictures."

When Dr. Mac has taken four different X rays, each from a different angle, she takes the film into the clinic to process it. When she comes out of the clinic a few minutes later, she looks relieved.

"No breaks, no fractures," she says. "I suspect that when the trailer was hit, it threw Trickster against the far wall. He hit his hock, which accounts for the bruising and cut. He must have lost his balance and twisted his hock a bit." She points to the injured joint.

"If he's hurt, then how could he run the way he did when he first got out of the trailer?" I ask.

"You have to understand a horse's personality before you make any medical diagnosis," Dr. Mac says. "This fellow strikes me as high-spirited. Would you say that's right, Lucas?"

Mr. Quinn pets Trickster's neck. "He's young, doesn't know his limits. Horses like this can injure themselves by pushing too hard. We have to make sure they don't do that." He turns to Dr. Mac. "How do you want to treat the leg?"

"Rest, cold packs, and some anti-inflammatory medicine," Dr. Mac answers. "I don't think you should coop him up in a stall. He'll go nuts. A moderate amount of gentle exercise—walking—will help."

"How are you going to get him back in the trailer?" I ask. "He didn't like it very much."

"I'll give him a mild sedative," Dr. Mac says. "That ought to calm him down."

"I could ride in the trailer with him," I offer.

Mr. Quinn grins. "No, I don't think so. The two of you locked in a small place like that, something is bound to happen. Wouldn't be safe."

"Still want us to follow you in the van?" Dr. Mac asks.

Mr. Quinn checks his watch. "It's already pretty late," he says. "Tomorrow's Saturday.

Bring the kids out early, and we'll put everyone to work then."

Trickster shifts his weight and bumps his shoulder against me. He likes me. I know I'm not making this up.

"Mr. Quinn, can I help you with Trickster?" I ask. "I mean, with the exercising Dr. Mac was talking about."

Trickster snorts, and my bangs are in my eyes again.

"Well," Mr. Quinn says slowly. "That's quite a bit of horse there." He rubs his hand over his buzz cut. "Let me think about it. We'll talk when you come out tomorrow."

Chapter Four

· · · · · · · · · · ·

The next morning, Dr. Mac turns the van past the wooden sign that reads "Quinn's Stables," and we bounce down the dirt road toward the barns.

I'm back!

Green pastures stretch out on both sides of the road, surrounded by white fences and filled with horses of every color and size—a jet-black Thoroughbred, spotted Appaloosas, a pair of matching Clydesdales, and many others. We ooh and aah at the beautiful animals grazing in the fields.

I feel like jumping out of the van and running the rest of the way. No, better not. Dr. Mac wouldn't like that. I'm working hard to stay on everyone's good side.

At the top of a long hill, we can finally see the stables—a collection of smaller buildings and sheds around a large, modern barn. The Quinns' house, a two-story stone building, sits off to the east. There is a pond beside it with a loud family of ducks splashing in the water.

Nothing has changed since the last time I was here. As I get out of the van, I take a deep breath. It even smells the same. Hay and horses, the best smells in the world.

A tanned woman wearing jeans and a white T-shirt walks toward us. She shakes hands with Dr. Mac.

"Good to see you again, Doc," she says.

"You, too," Dr. Mac replies. "I've brought your new stable hands."

"Pleasure to meet you all. I'm Linda," she says. "I've only been helping out here a few months, so I know what it feels like to be new."

"My name is David," I say, stepping forward. "This is Maggie, Brenna, Sunita, and Zoe. They've never been around horses before. But I have lots of experience."

"Excuse me?" Zoe says, stepping next to me. "I know how to ride. Mother sent me to horse camp in Connecticut last summer. I won first place in my age group."

"You?" I ask. "You never told me that."

"I don't like to brag about it," Zoe says.

"Oh, brother," Maggie mumbles.

"I've never been on a horse," Sunita tells Linda.

"Don't worry," Linda answers. "We have more than forty horses here, and one will be just right for you. Now, I'm going to take you on a tour, show you around a bit, then we'll put you to work."

Dr. Mac takes a plastic equipment case out of the van. "Lucas wants me to look at a sore leg and a hoof crack," she says. "I'll check in with you later."

As soon as she disappears into the barn, I nod to Linda. "I don't need the tour. I used to come here all the time. I'll help Mr. Quinn with Trickster while you get them started."

"Oh, no," Linda says with a smile. "Mr. Quinn was very specific. You're supposed to stay with the group and run a shovel this morning."

"What?" This is not what I had planned.

"He said something about you learning how to follow directions," Linda adds.

That sounds like something my mother would say.

"What does 'run a shovel' mean?" Sunita asks.

"You don't want to know," I say.

"You'll find out soon enough," Linda says. "Come on, let's get started." She leads us into the largest barn. "This is the newest building here. Mr. Quinn had it built five years ago."

"Does Mr. Quinn own all of the horses?" Zoe asks.

"He owns about half of them," Linda answers. "Six are his prizewinners, the horses he races or shows. The most famous one is Quinn's Starfire. He's won every prize there is to be won for a show horse on the East Coast."

"He probably cost more than my house," I add. "You wouldn't believe how expensive some of these horses are."

"The rest of Mr. Quinn's horses are the animals we use for lessons. The other twenty are boarders. They are owned by other people who pay us to take care of them."

"Were those the horses we saw when we drove in?" Sunita asks.

"Yep," Linda says. "We turn them out to the pastures in the morning while we clean the barn and get their feed ready. Then we bring them in for breakfast."

We follow Linda down the concrete aisle in the middle of the barn. Stalls line both sides of the aisle. Each stall is about twelve feet wide and ten feet deep, and each has a barred window that looks outside. Horses like to be able to see what's going on around them. Since all the horses are out grazing, the stalls are all empty.

We pass a teenage boy pushing a heavy wheelbarrow filled with straw and manure.

"Hi," he says briefly.

"That's Jared," Linda says. "I wish we had more like him. We can always use some extra hands to keep things clean, but we're desperate right now. It was really nice of you guys to offer to help."

Another stable hand comes toward us leading two old friends of mine, a tan-colored pony named Gus and an old gray spotted mare named Gertie.

"Gertie!" I say as I walk up to her and pet the side of her shaggy face. "How you doing, girl?"

I turn around and introduce her to the others. "Gertie was my favorite horse when I was a little kid."

"She's still a favorite around here," Linda says, shooing us to the side so Gertie and Gus can pass. "Follow me."

We stop again in the center of the barn, where a shorter hall crosses the long hall. Linda points up the shorter hall. "That's where you'll find the wash blocks—those are shower stalls for horses—the grooming stalls, feed room, cleaning supplies, and the office." She points to a wooden staircase. "The tack room, where we store saddle and riding equipment, is upstairs."

"What's down here?" Brenna asks, pointing to the other end of the short hall.

"That leads to the exercise ring," Linda says. "That's where your first lesson will start. Quinn told me that's the deal. You guys are getting riding lessons in exchange for helping out, right?"

Maggie and Zoe nod happily. Sunita and Brenna don't look as excited. They'll learn. I'll make sure they have a good time.

"OK, let's get you guys some shovels. Quinn wants you to clean out those dirty stalls we passed on the way in." She steps into the supply room and comes out with five shovels. "Manure-shoveling time!"

We troop back to the stalls at the far end of the barn.

"Every stall needs to be cleaned out," Linda says. "You'll notice that some of these stalls are pretty filthy. There's a couple of days' worth of mess in here. Dr. Mac says you guys are all hard workers, and this is where you get to prove it. David, since you have so much experience, why don't you show the others how it's done?"

This is not the topic I would have picked for show-and-tell, but I'm trying to do everything right today, even the gross stuff. I carry a shovel into the stall. The girls crowd around the door to watch.

"This is how you run a shovel," I say as I push manure and dirty straw to the front of the stall. I go back and scrape the rest of the floor clean until there is a heap of manure and straw at the stall door. "It's simple."

"You are very good at this, David," Sunita says with a straight face.

"Thank you," I say, trying to be dignified. "You have to clean the muck out of each stall and push it into the center aisle. Then somebody comes along and dumps it into a wheelbarrow. Pushing the wheelbarrow out to the manure pile is the worst job. Is Jared going to do that?" I ask Linda.

"Oh, no. He has to give a lesson. You are in charge of the dumping," she says with a wide grin. "Special request from Mr. Quinn."

"But..." Running the wheelbarrow is the worst job there is. It's heavy and smelly, and if the wheelbarrow tips over, you have to do twice the work.

Zoe's nose quivers. "Are you sure Gran knows that this is what we'll be doing?" she asks.

"You won't just be shoveling manure," Linda assures her. "You'll be cleaning tack—the bridles and saddles—feeding and watering the horses, bringing hay down from the loft, and cleaning up the courtyard."

Brenna looks strangely relieved. "Doesn't sound like there will be much time for riding," she says.

"Don't worry," Linda says. "There will be plenty. Quinn said you guys should work for a couple of hours, then we'll get you in the saddle."

It's impossible to keep up with four stall shovelers, even amateurs. When I fill the wheelbarrow, I have to push it outside, around the barn, past a toolshed, and through the parking lot to the manure pile. After the third trip, my arms feel like they are about to fall off.

They don't need me, they need a superhero—Manure Boy—to take care of this.

Wouldn't it be easier to train the horses to go to the bathroom in the manure pile? If you think about it, it's like the horses have trained us, or at least me. I'm the one running around dumping *their* messes.

"Hurry up, David!" "I'm done, David." "You missed a spot, David!" the girls call after me. They don't realize how hard this is.

Pushing the fourth load, I have to stop by the toolshed. My arms are stretching so far I'm going to look like an orangutan by lunchtime. And I've fallen way behind the girls. They're going to be finished riding by the time I'm done doing this. And I won't have any time to spend with Trickster.

There has to be a better way. If the manure pile were closer to the barn...

I check over my shoulder. No one is looking.

I dump the muck behind the toolshed. I'll deal with it later.

• • • • • • •

By the time Linda comes back an hour later, the stalls are all clean. "That wasn't so hard, was it?" she asks.

"You don't really want us to answer, do you?" Zoe asks wearily.

"Did you dump all the muck out back?" Linda asks me.

I nod once.

"Maybe you should check behind a truck or look under a rug," Brenna says. "David's the best corner-cutter we have."

Before I can think of a snappy reply, Linda steps between us.

"Good job. Now, I'll clean the shovels while you head up to the tack room. Find a helmet, safety vest, and gloves that fit, then meet me in the exercise ring. Your horses are waiting for you."

Zoe and Maggie dash off, pumped about riding. Brenna and Sunita follow behind, a little slower. I really want to ride, but I want to see Trickster first. I follow Linda to the wash block, where there are plenty of hoses and scrub brushes for cleaning up.

"How is Trickster doing?" I ask.

Linda points a strong stream of water at the dirty shovels. "The boss is down at his stall with Dr. Mac. You shouldn't bother them right now. He doesn't like to be interrupted when a horse is with the vet." She turns off the hose and hangs up the shovels. "Come on. Let's get your lesson started."

"Um, I'll be right with you," I say. "Can I meet you in the ring. I sort of have to go to the bathroom."

I can feel myself blushing. It's embarrassing to say that, even if it's a lie.

"You know where the bathroom is?"

I nod, trying to look desperate.

"Don't dawdle."

I wait until Linda heads up the stairs to the tack room, then I hurry down to the far end of the barn.

I have to see Trickster.

Chapter Five

. . . .

Dr. Mac and Mr. Quinn stand with their arms crossed as Trickster munches hay in his stall.

"How's his leg?" I ask, walking quietly up behind them.

Trickster lifts his head at the sound of my voice. He nickers and shakes his head so that his forelock flops from side to side.

"David! Didn't hear you coming," Dr. Mac says. "It should heal without any problems. The swelling is already down, and he isn't limping. I don't see any infection in his cut. His prognosis is excellent, I'd say."

"How soon can I ride him?" I can feel Mr.

Quinn watching me. "I mean, how soon before he can be ridden?"

"That depends," Dr. Mac says. "I don't want to turn him loose in a pasture. He might reinjure himself. But I don't like the idea of keeping him in a stall twenty-four hours a day, either."

Mr. Quinn puts out his hands. "I don't have the staff to walk him, J.J.," he tells Dr. Mac. "I'm training three horses, on top of caring for the boarders and getting my own horses ready for competition."

"You run a risk either way, keeping him stalled or letting him run," Dr. Mac observes.

Mr. Quinn slaps the dust off his jeans.

Trickster knows we're talking about him. He sticks his head out of the stall door for me to pet him. I move the stray hairs of his forelock out of his eyes. He looks me right in the eye. It's like looking in a mirror. It's weird, but I feel like he's trying to talk to me—to tell me what he wants.

"I'll walk him." The words pop out of my mouth before I know what I'm saying. "I'll come as soon as school gets out and I'll stay until dark. I'll even come in the morning, before school starts."

Dr. Mac's right eyebrow goes up to half-mast.

Mr. Quinn recrosses his arms over his chest.

"I know you, David Hutchinson," he says. "You want something. What do you get out of this?"

No use fooling around. "I get to ride him," I say bluntly. "I'll do whatever Trickster needs, and when he's better, you let me ride him. We'd be great for each other, I can tell."

Mr. Quinn picks up some strands of straw on the floor and tosses them in the stall. What is he thinking?

"David has helped at the clinic almost every day this spring," Dr. Mac says. "He does a good job for me. I think he deserves a chance."

"You'd have to walk him for forty-five minutes morning and night, and make sure he doesn't get too warm," Mr. Quinn says sternly. "You'd be responsible for telling me if the leg swelled up any, or if he limped or tripped."

"Of course," I say. "I'll do whatever you need me to do."

"It may take a few weeks," Dr. Mac points out.

"And you won't wander off like you did during that little incident last year?" Mr. Quinn asks.

"No, sir, I promise, Mr. Quinn, I swear. I've learned a lot since then."

He relaxes and chuckles slightly, then shakes his head. "You sure do remind me of your father, you know that?"

I don't know what to say to that. I know Mr. Quinn is, or was, good friends with Dad, but I don't like talking about my father to anybody.

"All right, we have a deal," Mr. Quinn says abruptly.

"We do?"

"You heard me. We have a deal. Prove yourself with Trickster, and you'll ride him." Mr. Quinn points a callused finger at me. "But no fooling around, understand? No shenanigans, promise?"

"I promise! Scout's honor! Cross my heart and hope to die! What do you want me to do first?"

Dr. Mac's eyebrow sinks back where it belongs. "This horse needs a walk. A nice, slow walk. Don't let him trot or kick up his heels. Just a walk."

"Now?" I ask.

"I want to fit him out with a better halter," Mr. Quinn says as he checks his watch. "You can walk him while the girls have their first lesson.

Follow them and watch how he reacts to the other horses. I don't know too much about his social skills yet."

"And when he's all better, I get to ride him," I repeat, just to make sure he wasn't fooling with me.

"If you take care of him properly, you can ride him."

Yee-haa! I did it!

• • • • • • • •

By the time I get to the exercise ring, the girls are standing next to their horses, all of which I recognize from last year.

Maggie is teamed with Gus, which is just as well because they are both on the short side. Zoe will ride Claiborne, a deep bay Thoroughbred with white stockings, or markings, on the lower part of his legs. Sunita is next to old Gertie, a perfect fit. Gertie will be gentle and slow. Brenna is standing next to Blitzen, a palomino mare. I've never ridden her, but she has a reputation for being stubborn, so she'll be a good match for Brenna.

There is one extra horse, Farrah, saddled and waiting for me. I'm disappointed for a second that I'm not going to get to ride, but that's OK. Trickster will leave Farrah in the dust when he's better. We're going to be great together. Wait 'til the others hear the news!

I climb on the gate next to the girls and holler, "HEY, I'M GOING TO RIDE TRICKSTER!"

Bad idea.

Blitzen snorts and skitters sideways. Brenna clutches at the reins, but Blitzen bumps into the rear end of Gertie, Sunita's horse. Gertie looks at Blitzen and lowers her head again. Nothing fazes Gertie.

"Everyone stay calm," Linda says in a quiet but powerful voice. She slowly walks up to Blitzen and says something to her. Brenna looks pale. I feel stupid. I should know better than to shout at a group of horses, especially when there are green riders around.

When Linda has Blitzen settled down, she walks back to the middle of the ring. "OK," she says to me. "No more stunts like that. There's some gear for you on that hay bale. Put it on and keep your voice down."

"Sorry, I was a little excited," I say as I climb down into the ring. "I'm not riding today. Mr.

Quinn is going to let me work with Trickster. He wants me to walk him while you guys ride."

"Lucky you," Linda says. "He looks like a fun horse. OK, let's get going. Ready, girls? Mount up."

Zoe mounts perfectly. She puts the toe of her left boot carefully in the stirrup so she doesn't poke her horse in the side. She hops straight up and freezes for an instant, so Claiborne can get used to her weight. Then Zoe swings her right leg over the horse's back. She pauses again, standing with a foot in each stirrup. It's not polite to plop down on a horse's back. Claiborne is totally relaxed, so Zoe sits lightly in the saddle.

Sheesh, she was telling the truth. She really has ridden before. But she can't call herself a real rider, not until she shovels a lot more manure.

Maggie struggles a little, but pulls herself up into Gus's saddle. Linda gives Sunita and Brenna boosts and shows them how to put their feet in the stirrups and sit so that their weight is forward, where it is most comfortable for the horse.

Once everyone is correctly seated, Linda stands in the middle of the large ring. "We're going to start out nice and easy. Gently squeeze your heels to tell your horse to walk."

The girls follow the instructions and their horses step forward. "Good, good," Linda calls. "Just walk nice and slow. Get to know your horse, and let your horse get to know you. Relax. Horses are extra-sensitive creatures. They can tell if you're nervous, if you're happy, if you feel sick, or if you are having the time of your life. Relax."

"Easy for her to say," Brenna mutters as she and Blitzen pass me. "She's standing on the ground."

If I didn't know any better, I'd say Brenna was nervous. But she's not afraid of anything, not even snakes, which—to be totally honest—make me want to scream and climb on top of furniture.

"You're doing great, Brenna," I call. "Chill out and you'll have more fun."

"It's not so bad," Maggie calls from the other side of the exercise ring. "When can we gallop?" She and Gus are moving along like they've been riding together for years. Maggie can do anything athletic.

Linda has the riders practice starting and stopping and lets them circle the ring a few more times. Then she opens the gate that leads outside and swings herself up onto her horse, a medium-sized bay with a white blaze down the middle of his brown face. I'm not sure about the breed. He has a heavy build. Maybe he has some Clydesdale blood in him. He wasn't built for speed, that's for sure.

"Time to head out on the trail," Linda says.

"The trail?" Brenna asks.

"Don't worry, you can do it," Linda assures her. "You look terrific. Here's the order I want. I'll go first, then Sunita, Maggie, Zoe, Brenna. David, you follow behind us leading Trickster."

While the others get in line, Brenna hangs back.

"Are you sure you don't want to ride? I could walk Trickster," she offers.

"Are you OK?" I ask quietly, so that the others can't hear. I've never seen Brenna nervous before.

"What do you mean? Of course I'm OK," she says quickly. "What? You think I'm afraid? I just thought you wanted to ride. You were so fired up about it at the clinic."

"Brenna, David—get it in gear," Linda calls.

"I'm not afraid of anything," Brenna mutters as she urges Blitzen forward.

I follow them out of the enclosed exercise ring to the paddock outside. Trickster is waiting for me at the gate with Mr. Quinn.

Trickster nickers loudly. I think he missed me.

"Here you go," Mr. Quinn says, handing me the lead rope. "Take it nice and slow, and there won't be any problems."

"Are you coming with us?" I ask.

"Nope, I'm going to put Starfire through his paces," he says, nodding toward the saddled horse.

Starfire, Mr. Quinn's best show horse, prances in place. A giant black Thoroughbred who can run faster than the wind, Starfire is the perfect horse for Mr. Quinn. They are both strong and smart.

"We'll be jumping in the field at the base of the hill," he continues. "Follow directions and be careful."

"Are we ready?" Linda calls from the head of the line.

"All set," I answer.

Linda's horse moves forward, followed by my friends.

Trickster picks up his feet quickly, like he wants to trot, but I put my hand on his shoulder.

"Oh no, you don't," I tell him. "We are not running today. You heard Mr. Quinn. Take it easy."

Trickster snorts loudly, as if he's annoyed. He feels like running. I can't blame him, especially after being cooped up in the trailer yesterday. And it's a perfect day—not too hot, not too cold. The grass is green, a breeze blowing…

Stop it. No running today. Pay attention to Trickster and watch his leg.

"Soon, buddy." I stroke his muzzle. "We'll get to run soon, I promise. But not today."

Chapter Six

● ● ● ● ● ● ● ● ● ● ● ●

The girls all look comfortable, even Brenna. Zoe has the best posture, and Maggie is sitting well, too. Sunita and Brenna are getting bounced around in the saddle a little, but that's OK. They'll learn how to move with the horse soon.

We climb the long hill behind the barns. Below us, I can see Mr. Quinn mount Starfire, and the two of them start their jumping exercises in the ring. He and Starfire look like they are one animal, like something out of a storybook—turning, cantering, leaping, and landing. That's what I'm going to look like when I ride Trickster.

Linda stops at the top of the hill, where the trail forks. One path continues up over the hill, and the other heads into the woods.

"Which trail are we going to take?" Maggie asks.

Linda points to the right. "We'll ride along the top of the hill, then down the other side. It's a gentle slope," she explains. "You can't take the wooded trail until you have more experience."

"When do we get to jump?" Zoe asks.

"Not today," Linda says, smiling. "Not for a while. Let's go."

She presses her heels into the sides of her horse and he steps forward. Maggie, Sunita, and Zoe's horses follow her. But Brenna's horse doesn't move. She flaps the reins. Blitzen stays put.

"Maybe you should say please," I tease, as Trickster and I walk toward them.

"You're no help," Brenna says.

"Use your legs," I say. "Give her a gentle squeeze."

"I'm trying. She won't go!"

"Move forward. You're sitting too far back in the saddle."

Brenna looks exasperated. "David, look at me. If I move up any farther I'll be sitting on her head! You're the big horse expert. Do something!"

As Trickster and I step closer, Blitzen flattens her ears and skitters sideways. She's staring at Trickster, swaying her head a little so she can get a good look at him.

"Hang on," I say. "I don't think Blitzen likes Trickster very much. He's making her nervous. Let me tie him up."

I lead Trickster a few steps away and look around for something to tie him to. There is nothing, unless you count a few patches of daisies. I could lead him across the field to the woods and tie him to a tree, but then I'd have to walk him to the woods, walk back, help Brenna, walk to the fence, get Trickster, and catch up with the group. It makes me tired just thinking about it.

"Go get Linda," Brenna suggests. "This isn't working."

"Don't worry. I can handle this," I say confidently. "Give me one second."

I lead Trickster farther away to a thick clump of grass. "Snack time, boy. Stay here and munch while I help Brenna."

Trickster snorts once and lowers his head to nibble hungrily. He's not going anywhere, not while he can eat.

"Are you sure he's going to be OK there?" Brenna calls.

"We understand each other," I say. "He listens to me. Now let's deal with Blitzen."

As soon as I get close enough to touch Blitzen, she nervously steps sideways again. "Well, that worked," I say. "She just likes to walk sideways, that's all."

"Be serious," Brenna says. "I don't want to go sideways. I want to go forward. Go get Linda."

Linda and the others are out of sight. They've already started down the other side of the hill.

"We don't need her. You just have a stubborn horse. It's a perfect match, if you ask me."

"Oh, ha," Brenna says with a scowl.

"You don't like this, do you?" I ask.

Brenna looks back down the hill to the show horses and barns.

"Are you afraid?" I ask.

"Yeah, kind of," she admits. "Don't you dare tell anyone."

"Cross my heart and hope to die," I say, crisscrossing my fingers over my shirt. "Your secret is safe with me. But there is nothing to be afraid of. You're doing fine. You just have to relax."

"Easy for you to say!"

"Come on, you're the nature queen. Be natural. Blitzen is acting weird because she doesn't know what you want her to do. Hold the reins loosely, look straight ahead, tell her to walk, and give her a little kick. Be confident."

Brenna takes a deep breath and picks up the reins. "I can do this, right?"

"Tell her what to do."

Brenna looks determined. "Blitzen, giddyup," she says with authority, squeezing her heels.

Blitzen takes a step forward, hesitates, then takes another step. And another.

"See? You did it all on your own!" I say, walking next to them.

Trickster looks up at us to see what's going on, then goes back to his snack.

Brenna grins. "Yeah, I did, didn't I?"

Maybe I could give lessons this summer. Teaching isn't that hard.

"Good job, Blitzen," I say, giving the horse a smack on the rump.

Big mistake.

Blitzen hunches her back and takes off like a shot for the woods, with Brenna bouncing in the saddle. It's like I set off a firecracker.

"Help, help!" Brenna cries. "DAVID!"

"Brenna!" I scream. "Pull back on the reins!"

"I can't!" she shouts. "DAVID!"

Blitzen is heading for the woods.

I spin around. Linda can't see us. We're alone. Trickster lifts his head, whinnies, and—

"NO!"

Trickster breaks into a gallop and takes off in hot pursuit of Blitzen. He looks like a turbo-charged horse, running like wildfire, his legs a blur. He thinks this is a race.

"HELP!" Brenna screams. One of her boots has slipped out of the stirrup and she has dropped the reins. Blitzen suddenly turns away from the woods. Trickster follows.

"Hang on!" I holler.

Brenna clutches onto the saddle horn with both hands. She is not balanced at all. If she falls she could break her neck! What do I do? I can't catch either horse. I can't leave to get help. Oh, no, this is all my fault!

"Help!" I scream loudly. "HELP!"

Blitzen swerves back the other way and heads

for the wooded trail again. Trickster quickly changes directions and stumbles. His leg! He's hurt it again. He keeps running, but not as fast as before.

"Pick up the reins!" I shout as Brenna vanishes into the woods. Trickster follows. No one is coming to help. I sprint toward the woods, trying to make my feet fly, ignoring the pain in my side. At least I'll be able to help Brenna if she falls. No, don't think that. She's not going to fall. She's not going to fall.

The trail turns sharply to the left as it enters the woods. *Keep running. Keep running.*

There they are!

Trickster is right behind Blitzen, chasing her down the trail. Brenna is still clinging to the saddle, but both of her feet are out of the stirrups now.

Suddenly, I hear hooves thundering behind me. I jump out of the way just in time for Mr. Quinn to rocket by on Starfire.

Chapter Seven

• • • • • • • • • • •

The black horse and rider whiz by me as they speed toward Brenna and Blitzen. Mr. Quinn leans close over Starfire's neck, urging him on. Starfire passes Trickster in a flash and pulls up alongside Blitzen.

Mr. Quinn leans over and grabs Blitzen's dangling reins, and Starfire hits the brakes and slows down. Blitzen strains for a second and then calms down. Both horses trot, then walk. Finally, they stop.

Brenna is safe! She gives Mr. Quinn a wobbly smile as he slips off Starfire's back. He holds Blitzen's head so Brenna can dismount.

Trickster has stopped running, too. Now that the race is over, he's ready to eat again. He has wandered off to sniff a patch of ferns, trying to decide if they would be tasty.

"Oh no, you don't," I say. "You're already in trouble. You don't want to get a stomachache on top of everything else."

I pick up the lead rope and start to walk him to Mr. Quinn, but he flinches and lifts his right hind leg.

"He's hurt it again, hasn't he?" Mr. Quinn demands harshly from the trail. "Strained the hock, maybe fractured something."

I don't know what to say.

"Stay where you are, David," Mr. Quinn orders. "Brenna, go on back to the other trail. I'm sure Linda is looking for you by now. Tell her today's lesson is over. I want the horses back in the barn, now."

"Um, sure," she says. "Thanks for helping me."

Brenna looks a little shook-up, but Mr. Quinn looks positively awful. His face looks like someone drained all the color out of it. All the friendliness, too. His jaws are moving like he's grinding his teeth, and his eyebrows are pulled down into a frown. I've seen that look before—when I got in trouble last year.

"Go on, Brenna," Mr. Quinn repeats. "I need to talk to David."

I don't like the way that sounds.

Brenna shoots me a look like she wishes she could help but can't, then she leaves. It only takes a minute until she's out of sight.

"I don't know what spooked Blitzen," I explain to Mr. Quinn, as he leads Starfire over. "Brenna got her walking and she just took off."

Mr. Quinn doesn't answer.

"Maybe she got stung by a bee or something."

Still nothing. Starfire shakes his head to shoo away a pesky fly. Trickster lifts his sore leg to take the pressure off.

Mr. Quinn hands me both Starfire and Blitzen's reins. "Hold on to these—tightly." Then he checks Trickster over, running his hands down the length of the leg. Mr. Quinn's so quiet it's making me nervous.

"How is he?" I ask. "Is he going to be OK?"

Mr. Quinn pats Trickster's back.

"I was stupid," he says.

"Excuse me?"

"I was stupid," he repeats, unbuckling his riding helmet. "I thought you were ready, that you had done some growing up." He runs his right hand over his short black hair. "Dr. Mac said you were reliable, and Trickster definitely took a shine to you. Horses have a good judgment. Usually."

He sets his helmet on the ground and tucks up the stirrups that hang from Starfire's saddle. "But I was stupid. You're not ready to be responsible around horses."

"Uh-oh. The *R* word—*responsibility*.

"You went barreling into the exercise ring hollering so loud I could hear you clear down at the end of the barn." I hold my tongue about that. "What if your carelessness had caused a horse to dump somebody?"

"But that didn't happen!"

He ties the riding helmet to Starfire's saddle. "No, but you slapped Blitzen's rear end. That did happen. I saw it. I was watching all of you head up the trail, thinking how good you were with Trickster. Then you let him graze without tying him to anything—"

"There was nothing to tie him to!" I interrupt.

"—and you spooked Blitzen. By the time I

was back on Starfire, those two animals were tearing toward the woods, and Brenna was in danger."

"But you make it sound like I did it on purpose. I was just patting Blitzen. I didn't mean to scare her. I had just shown Brenna how to make her walk. Blitzen's my friend. I would never do anything to hurt her."

"You were careless. You smacked Blitzen because you weren't thinking. You didn't tie Trickster properly. Why? Did it seem like too much work? Because you figured no one would find out?" He takes off his gloves and smacks them angrily on his jeans.

I feel like I just got kicked in the stomach.

"I'm sorry," I say. "I'm really sorry. I didn't mean for any of this to happen. I never thought..."

"That's it—you didn't think," Mr. Quinn says. Blitzen's ears twitch at the sound of his angry voice. "And people who don't think have no business being around horses. Now run to the barn and get Dr. Mac. I don't want to move Trickster until we wrap his leg."

I know I should do exactly what he says, without arguing, debating, or anything. But I have to ask.

"Mr. Quinn, what about our deal?" I ask. "Can I still ride him when he's all better?"

Mr. Quinn's eyes narrow, and he looks right through me.

"The deal is off."

Chapter Eight

· · · · · · · · · · · · ·

I really blew it this time. Major, big time, blew it. Mr. Quinn will never let me ride. He'll tell all the other stable owners. He'll tell everyone in the whole state not to let me near their horses. He'll run ads on the Internet. I'll never ride again.

I'm sunk.

Even though I'd like to run all the way home, I head for the barn. Dr. Mac is examining the hoof of a nervous filly in the barn.

"Back so soon?" she asks. "How was Trickster?"

"Not so good. Mr. Quinn needs your help. He's with Trickster, up in the woods."

She puts down the filly's hoof. "What happened? What's wrong?"

"He got away from me and ran. Hard. He hurt his leg again."

I can't say any more, but it doesn't matter. Dr. Mac grabs an equipment box and blows past me to see her patient.

"There you are," Zoe calls, her voice echoing down the barn. "Are you OK?"

The last thing I want to do is explain all this to the others. They're my friends and all, but it's going to make me look really stupid. I turn to walk out of the barn.

"David!" Zoe calls louder. She runs up to me and grabs my arm. "Brenna told us everything."

"I'm going to call and see if my mom's home," I say. "Maybe she can pick me up. I have to go."

"You can't go," Zoe says.

"I can't stay. Mr. Quinn won't let me ride. I'm a danger to horses. I mess up everything."

Zoe smiles gently. "You don't mess up everything. You just mess up... a lot. We'll work on it, don't worry. Now come on. We need your help grooming the horses."

Gertie, Claiborne, and Gus are waiting in the stalls, cross-tied and ready for grooming. Each horse stands between two wooden posts, with a rope attached to each side of its halter and a post. This will hold them steady so they can't walk away.

"Hey," I say quietly to the girls.

"Hey, yourself," Brenna says. "How are you? Did Mr. Quinn yell? He looked really angry."

"Brenna told us what happened," Sunita explains. "It was brave of you to try and help her."

"That's not how Mr. Quinn saw it," I say.

"He just needs to cool off a bit," Maggie says confidently. "It's like that time I fell out of the tree in my backyard. Gran was angry and worried all at the same time. Once she cooled down, she told me she was impressed that I climbed so high. Of course, I was still grounded for a week."

"That's not a helpful example," Zoe tells her cousin.

"Is so," Maggie replies.

"Let's not argue," Sunita suggests. "We're supposed to be grooming." She turns to me. "That's why we need your help. Linda started to show us what to do, but then she had to go help Jared."

"Something about some hay being delivered," Maggie says. "She told us to get started. It seemed easy enough watching her, but now we're not sure what to do."

"Zoe's been around horses before," I say. "At her summer camp."

"Well...it was a different kind of camp," Zoe explains. "Parents sent kids to ride, not to clean stables or give them baths."

"This isn't a bath, this is grooming," I correct.

"Whatever," Zoe says. "I can braid manes, though. My camp counselor showed me how to do that."

Zoe's horse, Claiborne, lifts his head. I'm sure he would love a braided mane, but I suspect he'd like all that trail dust off of him first. I might as well help them. That way I'll have done something right today.

"OK, well, I guess I'm giving a grooming lesson," I say as I pick up the body brushes on the shelf. "This is a body brush. You use it to brush the dirt off your horse. Start up on the neck and move the brush in the direction the hair grows," I say, demonstrating on Gertie.

"Then what?" Sunita asks.

"You do that down the whole body, first on the left side, then on the right."

The girls approach the horses and start brushing. "Use some muscle," I tell them. "If your arms don't get tired, then you aren't brushing hard enough."

"We have to brush the entire animal?" Zoe asks.

I nod my head. "The whole thing." It feels kind of cool to be the one giving directions. It's very nice not being yelled at.

When all four horses have clean, shiny coats, I show the girls how to use a facecloth to gently wipe around the horse's eyes, ears, and muzzle.

"Aren't we going to braid their manes?" Zoe asks.

"You don't really have to do that," I say.

"Of course we do," Zoe says firmly. "Claiborne is an elegant horse. He needs to look his best."

"I like braids," Maggie says.

I give up. "All right. We'll braid. Are you sure you know how to do this?" I ask Zoe.

She is scouting the equipment on the shelf. "We've got brushes, combs, and rubber bands here. We're all set. Hey—there's Trickster."

Everyone stops to watch as Mr. Quinn and

Dr. Mac walk Trickster past us. His hooves clop on the cement floor in an uneven rhythm. He is limping badly, trying not to put his weight on his sore leg.

My chest tightens. Here I've been feeling so rotten, so sorry for myself about getting yelled at and not being able to ride, that I didn't even think about Trickster. Mr. Quinn is right—I don't think.

"You guys stay here," I tell my friends. "I have to see how he's doing."

I swallow hard and follow Trickster down to his stall. It feels like I'm walking to the principal's office.

Once Trickster hobbles inside, Dr. Mac and Mr. Quinn notice me standing behind them. Mr. Quinn stares at me for a minute. "I'll be at the office," he tells Dr. Mac. He walks off without another word.

"He hates me," I say when Mr. Quinn is out of sight.

"Don't worry about Lucas," she says. "He has a lot of things on his mind right now."

She's just saying that to make me feel better. Like anything could right now. "What's going to happen to Trickster?"

Dr. Mac kneels to check the wrap on Trickster's leg. It has to be tight enough to support the joint, but not too tight or his blood won't flow properly.

"I gave him an injection for the pain. That should kick in soon. He'll be sleepy for the rest of the day, but the leg won't hurt as much."

"Is it broken?"

She shakes her head. He may have strained some tendons, though. We'll take the cold pack off in twenty minutes. He has to rest—total rest—for a few days. If the swelling doesn't go down, we'll take him to an equine clinic for an ultrasound exam. There's a chance he has torn the tendon. That would mean surgery."

"Will he have to be put down?" I ask quietly.

"Relax, David. It's not that bad. But it will be a while until we know if he's going to run again. Now, I have to get back to that sore hoof before we leave. Tell the girls to meet me at the van in half an hour."

I wait until she walks away before I look at Trickster. He nickers softly, but he doesn't bob his head or toss his forelock around.

"I'm sorry, buddy," I say.

Chapter Nine

• • • • • • • • • • •

David Alexander Hutchinson!" my mother shouts.

I freeze, halfway out of Dr. Mac's van.

"She doesn't sound too happy," Maggie says. "You'd better go home. We'll save you some pizza."

"Don't bother," I tell her. "I'm not very hungry."

"Man, you really are bummed," Brenna says.

I slip out of the van before anyone has a chance to answer, and meet my mother in the middle of the road. She doesn't say a word until we're in the garage. Then she lets fly.

"Do you know happened today?" she asks.

Mom is still wearing her suit and high heels from work. Her mouth is tight, like she just sucked on a lemon, and her eyes look like they could spit fire. I guess this is a bad time for a smart-mouth answer.

"No," I reply quietly as I open the door to the laundry room. We pass through piles of laundry—it's beginning to look like a mountain range—and step into the kitchen.

"You weren't here when I needed you," she says.

My five-year-old sister, Ashley, is eating a McDonald's feast at the kitchen table. My older brother, Brian, is nowhere in sight. He must be at work.

"When did you need me?" I ask, taking a french fry out of Ashley's cardboard container.

"Mom, he's stealing," Ashley tattles.

Mom slaps her hand on a piece of paper on the counter. "Here! Right here. Didn't you read this note? I put it where you would see it when you came down to breakfast."

She hands the note to me. It says I was supposed to be home by two o'clock so I could watch Ashley while Mom went into the office. I was also supposed to take out the trash and start the laundry.

"I never saw it," I say, telling the absolute truth. "I woke up late, really late. My stupid alarm clock didn't go off. I just grabbed a soda and a handful of pretzels and ran over to Dr. Mac's. She was pulling out of the driveway. I barely made it." I peer into the McDonald's bag on the kitchen table. "Did you get me any fries?"

Mom starts to hand me the bag, but then pulls it back. "You had soda and pretzels for breakfast?" She shakes her head as if she's clearing out the cobwebs. "No, wait, I'm not going to let you sidetrack me. You didn't return the messages I left for you yesterday at the clinic, and then you ignored the note today. I had to take Ashley into the office with me."

"Mom's office is boring!" Ashley says dramatically. "It was so boring I almost threw up!"

"It's not that bad," I say. "I used to go there when I was little. They have crayons."

"That's not the point," Mom says, sitting down. She kicks off her shoes and lets out a little sigh of relief. "I don't ask you to baby-sit often, but when I do, I need to be able to count on you."

"What about Brian?" I ask.

"Brian has his own job. He was there all afternoon and has an extra shift tonight."

She makes it sound like he's working in a coal mine or something. Brian has a cushy job at the movie theater. He runs the projector. Basically, he gets paid for watching movies and eating popcorn. I have to be nice to him so he'll give me the job when he goes to college. If he ever goes to college.

"He even called me to make sure it was all right for him to stay for the extra shift. That's the kind of responsibility I need from you."

I study an orange stain on the countertop. Juice, probably, or soda. I scratch the stain. It looks permanent. We may have to cover this one with the toaster.

"David? Are you listening to me?"

I can't do anything right today.

"I'm sorry, Mom. I didn't mean to let you down."

As soon as I apologize, her shoulders relax. "All right. Let's make sure it doesn't happen again." She hands me a container of fries. "How was the stable? Did you get to ride? I know you were excited."

"I don't want to talk about it." I look into the bag again. "Did you get any ketcup packets?"

"Did something happen?" Mom's shoulders tense up again.

"The stable was—it's just that Mr. Quinn has this new horse. Trickster. You should see him. He's fast as the wind! Dad would love him."

Mom checks her fingernails. Bringing up Dad is not a good thing to do, especially when she's tired.

"Anyway, this horse, Trickster—Mr. Quinn promised I could ride him. All I had to do was to help out with him for a few weeks because he has a sore leg."

"What happened?" Ashley asks. "Did he run away?"

"Well, to make a long story short, he hurt his leg again. Badly. I'm not going to be able to ride him for a long time, if ever. Mr. Quinn is pretty upset. So am I."

"I'm sorry, honey," Mom says gently. "That must be a terrible disappointment to you. But there are lots of other horses there."

"You don't get it," I tell her. "It's not the same. Trickster is the only horse I want to ride. It's like we're connected or something. Like we understand each other, speak the same language." I put down the fries. "Mr. Quinn hates me, Mom. He thinks I'm an idiot. He doesn't want me around Trickster. He doesn't want me around, period."

"What about tomorrow?" she asks. "I thought you guys were going to be helping at the stables on the weekends for a while."

I shake my head. I really want to see Trickster, to help him recuperate, but I can't. Mr. Quinn's lecture is still echoing in my head. I don't want to get another one of those anytime soon.

"I'm staying home tomorrow," I say.

Mom crosses the kitchen to the giant calendar that hangs next to the telephone. "OK. It will help me if you do. I have to spend the morning at the office, catching up on paperwork. You can watch Ashley. You owe your sister something special, since you let her down today."

"What?" I ask wearily.

Ashley jumps in her seat. "I want a tea party!"

Chapter Ten

• • • • • • • • • • •

Tea parties are cruel and unusual punishment. But I'm stuck. Mom taped a giant note to the refrigerator that I couldn't miss: "I'll be back at noon. Take out trash and start some laundry. Tea party outside!"

Smart lady, my mom.

The trash and laundry can wait. I want to get this party over with. Maybe it will keep my mind off Trickster.

I move the yellow plastic picnic table to the front lawn and bring a folding chair for me. Ashley doesn't really want tea, so I pour lemonade into one of her plastic teapots. I can't find any teacups. They're probably buried in the sandbox. Paper cups will do. Last but not least, I carry the entire cookie jar outside and bring a roll of paper towels, just in case.

All right, it's party time.

"Ashley!" I yell.

My sister peers out the screen door, then opens it and studies the setup from the front porch. She's wearing her Cinderella costume from last Halloween over a pair of Tweety slippers, and she has a dishcloth on her head for a veil.

"You're not dressed right," she says with a pout.

"What do you mean?" I ask, checking my Philadelphia Flyers jersey for stains. "What's wrong with this?"

"I want you to be a clown," she says. "Like you were at my birthday party."

"No way, Ash. You didn't say a circus. You said a tea party. Look!" I pour lemonade into one of the cups and pick it up with my pinky finger sticking out. "I made pretend tea." I drink with my nose all scrunched up. I guess that's what you do at a tea party.

Ashley's lower lip sticks out farther, and she frowns. Uh-oh. Better do something quick or she's going to blow.

"OK, I'll be a clown. Give me a second."

"And I don't want pretend tea," she commands. "I want punch."

"Yes, your majesty," I mutter, trotting obediently back into the kitchen.

I pour the punch mix into a pitcher, set it in the sink, and turn on the water... Trickster has been fed and watered by now. I wonder if he's well enough to walk a bit. Is the swelling down? What if his leg got worse last night?

I have to stop thinking about him. Get a grip. It's time to be a clown.

The clown costume is in the bottom of the toy chest in the family room. I stick on the nose and wig, and take off my sneakers so I can put on the big floppy shoes. There used to be a matching shirt and pants, but they've disappeared, thank heavens. I hope Mom appreciates this at allowance time.

"David," Ashley calls from the front yard. "Hurry up!"

"Ta-da!" I shout, leaping onto the front porch.

Ashley looks skeptical. "Where are Baby Sally and Tigger and Oscar?"

"We're not having a tea party with your stuffed animals, Ash," I say. "It's just you and me and a ton of cookies—chocolate chip!"

"I want my friends," she demands, with her hands on her princess hips.

"I'm not going to eat cookies with a bunch of stuffed animals," I say.

"I'll tell Mom."

Ooh. She's getting tough.

Laughter erupts across the street. Maggie, Zoe, Brenna, and Sunita are standing at the end of the clinic driveway, pointing their fingers and laughing like this is the funniest thing they ever saw.

"Very funny," I say loudly. "Laugh it up, go ahead. I'm just trying to be nice to my sister."

They cross the street for a closer look.

"That hair is so you, David," Zoe says.

"I like the shoes," Brenna says, her shoulders shaking.

My face feels as red as this stupid wig.

"Would you like some tea?" Ashley asks her new guests in a dignified tone.

"I'd love some," Sunita says as she kneels in the grass next to the picnic table. Ashley pours

Sunita a tiny cup of lemonade and hands it to her. "Thank you very much," Sunita says politely.

"Don't encourage her," I say. I explain why I ended up doing this dumb party. "I just want to get this over with as soon as possible."

"Are you coming with us to the stables?" Brenna asks.

"When?"

Maggie takes another cookie out of the jar. "Mr. Quinn will be here to pick us up any minute now. I called you this morning and left a message. Didn't your mom tell you?"

"No," I say slowly. I bet she did that on purpose.

"Hey, where's the entertainment at this party?" Brenna asks. "You know how to juggle. I've seen you do it in the cafeteria at school."

"All right. One juggling clown, coming up." I grab a handful of cookies from the jar. I toss three, then four in the air, moving my hands quickly to keep them all going.

Ashley and our guests applaud. I toss the cookies high and catch one in my mouth. The others drop to the ground.

"Thank you, thank you," I say, bowing deeply.

A horn beeps as a blue pickup pulls into the driveway. It's Mr. Quinn.

"You kids ready?" he calls. The girls scramble to their feet and pile into the truck.

I should say something—anything—to Mr. Quinn. "How's Trickster?" I ask.

"Improving. A bit." Mr. Quinn pushes up the brim of his baseball cap to get a better look at me standing here in my red wig, fake nose, and floppy shoes.

"Can I watch a video?" Ashley asks, tugging on my jeans.

"Sure, go ahead."

"Seen your dad recently?" Mr. Quinn asks as he watches Ashley run into the house.

"Not for a while," I say. "He travels a lot. For his job. His new job."

"Hmmm. You usually wear that getup?"

"No, it's for Ash. I'm baby-sitting. Pretty lame, huh?"

"Not really," Mr. Quinn says. "It's good that you help your mom. I bet she counts on you a lot."

"Yeah, I guess she does." My cheeks feel like they're going to burst into flames.

Ashley opens the front door and screams at the top of her lungs, "The kitchen has a flood, David! You left the water on!"

"Uh...got to go, Mr. Quinn." Why do I always look like such a loser in front of him?

Mr. Quinn looks like he might say something, but he keeps his mouth shut. Shaking his head, he turns the key in the ignition and drives away.

He thinks I'm a complete idiot.

• • • • • • •

The kitchen is mopped dry by the time Mom comes home. I'm trying to recover from all the work by eating the cookies left over from the tea party. Mom gets out of the car and joins me at the picnic table on the front lawn.

"You look so cute!" she squeals. "But where's the guest of honor?"

"Ashley went to Jackie's house. She dumped me. Want some lemonade?"

Mom shakes her head. "No, thanks. There's some punch in the refrigerator."

Great. If I had known that earlier, the kitchen wouldn't have turned into a swimming pool. It took all the towels we own to clean up the mess.

"I washed the towels," I say. "I'll get the rest of the laundry going when they're done."

"It looks like you did a great job," she says enthusiastically. "I'm sorry I couldn't get home earlier. Do you want me to drive you to Quinn's?"

"Yes—I mean, no," I say. I want to visit Trickster, but I can't get the disappointed look on Mr. Quinn's face yesterday out of my mind. "Never mind."

"Why not?"

"It doesn't matter. I'm not going," I say.

"Doesn't matter? Horses don't matter to you? Since when?"

Here we go, twenty questions.

"I saw Mr. Quinn a little while ago. He thinks I'm a goofball."

"No, he doesn't, David. He let you come back and help him again."

I shake my bangs so they hang in front of my face. "I don't want to talk about it."

Mom reaches for a cookie. "Something is up. I know it."

"I said I don't want to talk about it. Any of it. I'm going to the clinic."

Chapter Eleven

. . . .

Oh, good, you're here," Dr. Mac says absently as I walk into the clinic. The waiting room is empty, and she's reading something on the computer.

"Mom just got home."

"I saw the little party you put on. That was a very sweet thing to do. Your sister will always remember that."

"That's what I'm afraid of."

Dr. Mac looks over the top of her bifocals at me. "Why didn't you go with Lucas and the girls?"

"Mom wasn't home yet. I couldn't leave Ashley alone." Both good excuses.

"I'm headed out there just as soon as I finish with the next patient. It's that ferret again, Rascal. You can ride with me if you want. I need to check Trickster's leg."

"I don't think Mr. Quinn wants me out there."

"Suit yourself." Dr. Mac stands up with a folder in her hand. "I have to work on my column. It seems like there's a deadline every time I turn around. Let me know when Rascal gets here."

Dr. Mac writes a newspaper column that runs in papers all over the country. She's not famous enough to be recognized in airports, but you'd be shocked at how many people know her name.

"What do you want me to do?" I ask.

She points to the balls of dog hair around the base of the potted plant. "Why don't you unearth the broom and dustpan? This floor is atrocious. Looks like it hasn't been swept in a month."

Oops.

As soon as she walks down the hall, I kick the fur balls under the chair. It's too quiet here. It feels weird without the others around.

I wonder what they're doing now. I bet they're still cleaning stalls. Who's going to dump the wheelbarrow? Brenna, probably. She's the strongest. She'll probably take the manure all the way back to the manure pile and not dump it behind the toolshed. That was another stupid thing I did yesterday. Mr. Quinn is going to find it, and he'll know it was me. Darn it, why do I do stupid things like that?

The bells on the front door jangle, jolting me out of my thoughts. It's the ferret guy, Erik, carrying Rascal's cage and looking stressed.

"I called Dr. MacKenzie," he says. "Is she here?"

"Here I am," Dr. Mac says calmly as she walks down the hall from her office. She lifts the reception counter and enters the waiting room. "Oh, Rascal," she says as she peers in his cage. "What have you done now?"

"He was in the drawer," Erik says. "I don't know how he got in there. I didn't see him. He was hiding. It's his paw. It's really smashed."

Dr. Mac puts on her glasses. "That would explain the blood. We need to take a look at this. Let's go into the Doolittle Room," she says, standing up and showing him into one of the exam rooms. "David, I'll need your help. Come on in and wash your hands."

As I scrub away, Dr. Mac takes Rascal's cage

and sets it on the examination table. "What's the first thing I need to do here, David?"

"Um…" I stall by putting more soap on my hands. I've never helped with a ferret before. "Take his temperature?"

"Good guess, but not yet."

"Check his heart?"

"Even before that," Dr. Mac says.

Three strikes and I'm out. Got to get it right this time. I turn off the water an dry my hands on a paper towel. "I know! You have to take him out of the cage."

"Very close," says Dr. Mac. "The first thing we need to do is close the door and make sure the cupboards are latched. It's hard to treat a patient you can't find. Ferrets can squeeze through openings only an inch wide."

Once I've locked everything up tight, Dr. Mac opens the cage door. Rascal slinks out onto the cool surface of the table. He isn't as perky as the last time we saw him. His eyes are half closed, and he doesn't try to run around at all.

Yikes. His front paw is a mess, swollen and bloody.

"That looks painful," Dr. Mac says. "What happened? Exactly."

Erik looks nervous. "It was my fault this time," he says. "I left my sock drawer open. Rascal loves socks—he must have gotten in there. When I went in the bedroom later, I slammed the drawer shut without checking."

"Hmmm," Dr. Mac says, slipping on her bifocals.

She gently scoops up Rascal, cradling him in her arm. She pets him gently, but I can see she's checking him out at the same time. She feels along his backbone and tail, then frowns. She moves her fingers along the bones in each one of his legs until she's ready to examine the paw.

Rascal pulls back and squeaks in pain.

"I know, I know, that hurts," Dr. Mac tells Rascal as she strokes his head to calm him down. "When did he injure his tail?"

"His tail? There's nothing wrong with his tail," Erik answers quickly. "Is there?"

"Well, the fact that it's not moving would be the first sign, plus there is some swelling. My guess is that it's broken."

"But how?"

"Think," Dr. Mac says. "When you've been playing with him, has he gotten his tail pinched in anything?"

Erik's face turns bright red. He has *guilty* stamped all over his forehead.

"You *have* been playing with him, haven't you? We talked about this a few days ago. Ferrets need time and attention."

"I've been busy," he confesses. "And he's so hard to catch. I can barely find him half the time. When I sat down in the recliner last night, he screamed and took off. He had been hiding in the chair. Freaked me out."

Dr. Mac stops petting Rascal. "You have a recliner?"

"An old one."

"Recliners are death traps for ferrets. They love to take naps underneath them. When someone leans back in the chair, they can be killed. Rascal is a quick fellow. I bet he broke his tail trying to get out of there."

"Oh, man," Erik says. "This wasn't supposed to be so hard. The guy who sold him to me said he was the easiest pet in the world."

Dr. Mac pauses, like she's searching for just the right words. Her right eyebrow is way up on her forehead.

"If you want an easy pet, a ferret is a bad idea," Dr. Mac says. "I need to do some X rays, but I'm pretty sure that Rascal has a broken tail and some broken bones in his paw."

"Is that going to be expensive?" Erik asks. "If he keeps costing me money, I'm going to have to get rid of him. Maybe I should just turn him loose."

What!? How can he say that? He doesn't care about Rascal at all.

"I have a better alternative," Dr. Mac says. "I know a woman who runs a rescue shelter for ferrets in situations like this. You pay for the X rays, and I'll arrange for Rascal to go to the shelter. Fair?"

He hesitates for an instant, then says, "All right."

• • • • • • •

"What a moron," I say after Rascal's owner— his former owner—has gone. "What an idiot, what a rat! Can you believe that guy?"

Dr. Mac puts Rascal into a roomy cage and closes the door. "You seem surprised."

"Of course I'm surprised. Aren't you? He thought it would be easier to dump Rascal than to take care of him! That's... That's..." I can't think of a word strong enough. Where's Sunita when I need her?

"That's *irresponsible?*" Dr. Mac asks, as she adjusts the water bottle hung from Rascal's cage.

"Way more than irresponsible," I protest.

Dr. Mac writes a note in Rascal's file. "When taking care of Rascal got boring, he took the easy way out. It happens all the time. Drives me nuts." She slaps the file closed. "Know what I mean, David?" she says pointedly.

I nod my head slowly. She's talking about me.

"You have been known, on occasion, to cut corners, too."

"But I would never do something to hurt an animal the way that guy did."

Rascal's cage rattles as he limps over to take a drink.

"What about Trickster?" Dr. Mac points out.

Ooh—that hurt.

I slump on a stool. "I know. I keep trying not to think about it, but it won't go away. How can I explain this, Dr. Mac? It's like there's a piece of me that I can't stand, the corner-cutting part. I start doing things and then, they're boring, or it takes too long, and I...just...stop."

"It's too bad you can't take that piece out."

"Exactly! Like a sliver or a wart. A big, ugly wart. But it doesn't work that way, does it?"

"You already know the answer to that. Maybe you need to grow a new piece, a 'do-things-right' piece."

I spin around once on the stool.

"I was responsible today, taking care of Ashley. I sort of flooded the kitchen, but I cleaned it all up."

"All of it?"

"All of it." I get up and follow Dr. Mac to the file cabinets behind the reception desk. "Honest. When I wanted to quit, I kept thinking about Trickster, how my corner-cutting hurt him. Not that me cleaning the floor would help him. I guess that's stupid, isn't it?"

"Not really," she says as she opens the file drawer. "Seems like it's all connected, if you ask me."

The phone on the desk rings, and Dr. Mac picks it up. "Veterinary clinic," she says crisply. "Lucas?" She pauses. "When did it happen? Have you taken his temperature?"

"What's wrong?" I ask. "Is it Trickster?"

She motions for me to be quiet. "I'll be right

there. Don't get upset. It's probably nothing, just a little colic."

I can't stand this.

"We're on our way," she says.

"What?" I ask as she hangs up.

"Quinn has a sick horse."

"Trickster?"

"No—it's Starfire."

Chapter Twelve

• • • • • • • • • • • •

Dr. Mac drives without a word, pushing the van above the speed limit once we get out of town. At first I was pumped about going with her and seeing Trickster, but the closer we get, the more I wish I had stayed at home. What if Mr. Quinn kicks me out of the barn?

"Maybe I'll just stay in the van," I say as we turn down the lane to the stables.

"Fine," Dr. Mac says, driving fast enough to create a cloud of dust behind us.

"Or I could just find the girls and, you know, steer clear of Mr. Quinn."

Dr. Mac hits the brakes, and the van skids to

a stop behind the barn. "Do what you want, David." She grabs two equipment boxes out of the back, slams it shut, and jogs into the barn.

I wish I had the guts to follow her. I want to see how Trickster is doing. I owe him an apology, too. If I had tied him up the way I should have, he'd be fine by now. We might even be out riding together.

I feel like a pile of manure just thinking about it. No—I don't want to go in the barn.

I sit on the bumper of the van. If my dad were here, he'd tell me to march right into the barn and deal with what's bugging me. "Get back on the horse when you fall off" was one of his big mottoes. It was easier to do when he was around. Everything was easier when Dad was around.

"Come on, boy, you can do it."

It takes a second to realize where the voice is coming from. It's Mr. Quinn, talking to Starfire as he slowly leads the horse into the courtyard. Dr. Mac is behind them, watching closely.

Starfire looks like a different horse from the one who rescued Brenna yesterday. His head and tail are down, and he walks slowly. He stops suddenly, jerking at the rope held by Mr. Quinn, and swings his head back toward his belly.

No wonder Dr. Mac was in such a hurry to get here! Starfire is Mr. Quinn's favorite horse—his most expensive one, too. If anything happens to him...

"See, this is what I was telling you about," Mr. Quinn says. "His belly is sore."

Starfire shakes his head and takes a few steps forward.

"Has he been rolling around in his stall?" Dr. Mac asks.

Mr. Quinn shakes his head. "Not that I've seen."

"Still, it could be colic," Dr. Mac says. "The symptoms point to it."

"That's what I thought at first, too," Mr. Quinn says. "But he's not having any trouble going to the bathroom. He's had diarrhea for the last hour. Do you think it's colitis X—that disease that kills racehorses?"

"Relax. I doubt that's it," Dr. Mac says. "That's pretty rare. I'd suspect a lot of other things first. Let's get him in a stall. I'll start an I.V. to replace the fluids he's lost. Where can we put him so he's isolated from other horses?"

"How about the foaling barn?" Mr. Quinn

asks as he strokes Starfire's back. "It's empty now."

"Great," Dr. Mac says. "If he has a virus, or something contagious, we don't want it to spread to the other horses."

That doesn't sound good.

"Come on, Starfire." Mr. Quinn leads the sick horse across the courtyard. Starfire stops suddenly and whinnies loudly, his neck arching up and his hooves pawing at the ground. While Mr. Quinn is distracted, I slip into the barn to check on Trickster.

My footsteps echo on the cement. The barn is clean and empty, the stalls all mucked out, with hay waiting in the hay nets for when the horses come in from the pasture. The girls must have worked really hard to get all the chores done.

I walk faster.

A familiar whinny comes from a nearby stall.

It's Trickster.

"Hi," I murmur as I walk toward the stall. "How are you doing? How's the leg?"

Trickster bobs his head up and down. His sore leg is wrapped to keep the swelling down, and he's still not putting weight on it. As I lean over the stall door, Trickster whinnies again and knocks over his empty water bucket with his nose.

Not only is his water bucket empty, but hay from the hay net is spread all over the stall, and the floor has a lot of manure and urine on it. Yuck. Not a nice place to recuperate in.

"What happened? Did the girls forget about you?" I can't believe they missed Trickster's stall. That wouldn't have happened if I'd been here. "Come on, boy—we've got to get this place cleaned up."

First, I lead Trickster into the aisle and tie his lead rope firmly to a metal ring on the stall door so he can't run off. Then I grab a shovel and wheelbarrow from the supply room and quickly clean the stall floor. Once the stall is clean with fresh straw on the floor, I fill the water bucket.

When I lead Trickster back into the stall, he immediately takes a long drink of water. He lifts his head, shakes his forelock, then drinks again.

"Thirsty, huh?"

He lifts his head for another breath of air, then puts his entire nose back in the water. I've never seen a horse drink that way before.

"What are you doing, you goofball, learning how to swim? You are the strangest horse I ever met. Take it easy, there. If you drink too fast, you could get a stomachache."

I reach for Trickster's halter to distract him. How long has he been without water? I gently tug his face toward mine so I can straighten his forelock. Wait a minute...what's this?

Trickster has strange bumps on his lips. They look like blisters—small, clear, and tender.

"I don't think these are supposed to be here," I tell the horse. "What have you been doing?"

Trickster snorts and pulls away from me. His ears flick toward the aisle of the barn. Then I hear footsteps. Someone is coming. Good. If it's Dr. Mac or Mr. Quinn, I want them to see this.

"Hello?" I call, sticking my head out the stall door.

"David!" Maggie says. "What are you doing here?"

The girls are leading their horses in single file behind Jared.

"Hey, how come you guys went riding before you cleaned Trickster's stall?" I ask.

Jared looks puzzled. "We didn't. We cleaned everything before we left."

When I describe the condition of Trickster's stall, he shakes his head.

"No way, man. I cleaned that one out myself. And I gave him water."

That sounds like the kind of excuse I'd give if I were caught not finishing a chore.

"Whatever," I say. "I took care of it. But I think something is wrong. Trickster has bumps by his mouth. They're really weird."

Jared frowns. "He's probably been chewing on his stall. Horses do that when they're bored. I'll go get the doc to look at him. Can you help the girls groom their horses? Just a quick brushdown. These critters were acting a little antsy on the trail. I think they want something to eat and a nap." He shakes his head. "What a day."

"OK," I say warily. There certainly seems to be something strange in the air today.

Chapter Thirteen

• • • • • • • • • • •

It takes a while to get the horses into the grooming stalls because they're all acting ornery. Gertie won't budge unless you push her, Gus keeps dropping his head, and Claiborne wants to kick anything that gets too close.

"Jeez," I say. "What did you do to these guys?"

Zoe takes off her riding helmet. "You mean what did they do to us? It was the strangest ride I've ever been on! Start. Stop. Start again. Stop. Walk two feet. Stop."

Brenna takes a brush off the shelf and starts to brush down Elsa, her horse. "It was the perfect pace, if you ask me. And Elsa was a lot easier to handle than Blitzen was."

"If you went so slow, then why are they sweating so much?" I ask. "It looks like they were racing."

Sunita gently strokes Gertie's neck. "I think that's why Jared brought us back early," she says. "He said they looked stressed, though he didn't know why. When we got close to the barn, he made us get down and walk."

"You walked them back?" I ask.

"Whoa, girl," Sunita says as Gertie stamps the cement impatiently. The old horse flares her nostrils and breathes fast. I've never seen her do that before.

"How long has she been breathing like this?" I ask as I reach for her halter.

"I'm not sure," Sunita answers. "She was OK when we started, and then she started breathing rapidly like this."

"The other horses are acting weird, too," Zoe adds. "Even Claiborne."

She pats his back, and Claiborne raises his hind foot to kick.

"Yikes!" Zoe says as she scoots out of the way. Instead Claiborne kicks his leg up toward his stomach. Next to him, Elsa paws the ground anxiously.

"Maybe there's a bug or something going around," I say. "Starfire is definitely sick. Dr. Mac put him in isolation in the foaling barn. Gertie?"

Suddenly, Gertie coughs. The old mare's body is quivering. Her eyes roll up in their sockets. Her legs shake. Gus and Claiborne snort and twist their heads, pulling on the cross-ties. Elsa whinnies.

Then Gertie's front legs buckle. "Oh, no!" I shout. "Get out of the way, Sunita!"

As soon as it starts, it's over. Gertie stops shaking and collapses to the floor, her legs folding under her. Her neck is stretched at an awkward angle. Her halter is still attached to the cross-tie ropes. Claiborne shrieks in distress and rises up on his hind feet.

"She's going to choke! Here, help me!" I grab Gertie's heavy head and try to release the cross-tie. "Brenna, help!"

"I'll get Dr. Mac," Sunita shouts.

Brenna helps me hold Gertie's head while Maggie and Zoe fumble with the cross-ties.

"Lift the head higher!" Maggie says.

Brenna and I strain. Gertie better not wake up or we'll all be in trouble.

"There!" Maggie says as she and Zoe release the cross-ties at the same time. Gertie's head and neck suddenly sag, and we lower her to the floor.

"Is she...?" Zoe asks.

I feel for the pulse under Gertie's jaw just like I've seen Dr. Mac do. "No, but her heart is racing."

"What happened? What's going on?" Dr. Mac asks as she runs up and kneels next to me.

"She was breathing hard and started shaking," I say. "The other horses are acting weird, too."

"Back up, everyone," Dr. Mac says. "You, too, David—move away."

We stand in the aisle as Dr. Mac listens to Gertie's heart and lungs with a stethoscope. She moves down Gertie's body, listening to her belly, too. Gertie's eyelids flutter, and she thrashes her legs.

"Look out, she's waking up!" Maggie says.

Dr. Mac scoots out of the way as Gertie struggles to her feet. The horse looks dazed, like she's not sure where she is.

Dr. Mac grabs her halter to keep her still. "It's

OK, girl, you're safe." She turns to us. "I want to get her out to the paddock by the foaling barn. Any horse acting strange should be brought out there. How are these guys?" she asks, pointing to Gus, Claiborne, and Elsa.

"They're not right," I answer quickly. "I think they're sick."

Dr. Mac points at Maggie. "I want you kids to wait by the van. I'll call someone to come and take you home."

"But—" Zoe starts.

"No buts, Zoe. You don't have enough experience being around horses to help here. It's one thing to help with an injured cat or dog, quite another when we're dealing with a thousand pounds of horse." Dr. Mac is not fooling around.

The others take off, but I stay with Dr. Mac. She takes the cell phone out of her equipment box and punches in a number, tapping her foot impatiently as she waits for the connection to go through.

"Let me stay," I ask. "I can help—you know I can."

Dr. Mac holds up one finger. "Yes, hello," she says into the phone. "Gabe? It's J.J. Get down to

Quinn's—stat! We have a situation here. Starfire is having heart problems, another horse just had a seizure, and we have a couple of cases that look like colic. Yes, it's ugly. Hurry."

"What is it, Dr. Mac?" I ask as she puts the phone away. "What's happening?"

"I don't know yet—some kind of strange viral infection, something in the water, or it could be a plant they ate in the pasture. I just hope we can figure it out in time," she says grimly.

"You don't mean ..."

"Yes, I do. This is serious, David. These horses might be dying. Now go with the others. There is nothing you can do to help around here, and I would feel better if you were home."

It takes a second for everything to sink in... Gertie's seizure, Starfire's heart problem, all the horses acting weird. Then it hits me like a hammer.

"Dr. Mac, I think Trickster's in trouble, too!"

Chapter Fourteen

· · · · · · · · · · ·

We find Trickster writhing on the ground in his stall, rolling in pain. His coat is sweaty and covered with bits of straw and manure. The stall that I just cleaned—what, half an hour ago?—is already a mess again. It smells really awful, not at all like regular horse manure.

"Trickster!" I shout.

He twists his head around toward us, then tries to get to his feet, but freezes when he's half-way up. He looks like he's sitting up like a dog.

C'mon, buddy. Stand up.

"Classic colic sign," Dr. Mac says. "His stom-ach is hurting him something awful. If he sits like that, it makes him feel a little better. What we don't want is for him to roll around on the ground. That could make his intestines twist. Horses can die from that."

Trickster slowly gets on his feet, his back legs shaking. His eyes roll back in his head as his belly spasms.

"Let's get him out of there," Dr. Mac says. "Walking can make a colicky horse feel better."

"But what about his leg?" I ask.

"That's the least of his problems right now. Help me here."

Dr. Mac enters Trickster's stall, clips a rope to his halter, and leads him out. Trickster steps gingerly on the concrete.

"Walk ahead of us," Dr. Mac says. "He'll follow better if he can see you."

We slowly make our way through the barn, Trickster's lopsided clip-clopping noise on the floor reminding me of his injury.

• • • • • • • •

The paddock outside the foaling barn looks like a hospital waiting room, except the patients have four legs and long tails. Gertie, Gus, Claiborne, and Elsa wander in the paddock, their heads low and necks dark with sweat. Jared sits on the fence keeping an eye on them. Through the foaling barn door, I can see Mr. Quinn talking to Starfire.

"J.J.," he calls to Dr. Mac. "I think his fever is going up."

"Claiborne keeps urinating," Jared says.

"Where should we put Trickster?" I ask.

"Too many horses, not enough hands," Dr. Mac mutters. She takes a deep breath. "OK, here's what we're going to do. We can't let them walk around the paddock. I want you two to take each of these horses into a foaling barn stall."

As soon as we bring the first horse, Claiborne, into a stall, Dr. Mac starts examining him. Dr. Gabe arrives, pulling his car around the side of the barn. He jumps out and starts unloading supplies. Dr. Mac and I run over to help.

"Did you get everything?" asks Dr. Mac.

"Everything you asked for and a few things you didn't," Dr. Gabe says, grinning as usual. He hustles a cooler of intravenous fluid and medicine into the barn.

With two vets, the examinations go quickly. They check the vital signs—temperature, respiratory rate, and heart rate—of each horse. Dr.

Gabe presses his stethoscope against Trickster's chest. "Seventy-two beats a minute," he says.

That's way too high. A normal pulse rate for a horse is thirty-five to forty beats a minute.

"It's got to be more than colic," Mr. Quinn says.

"The stomach pain looks like colic," Dr. Mac says, "but they all have diarrhea, so everything is flowing through their intestines well. Too well."

"They're dehydrated," Dr. Gabe observes.

"They've been drinking, but it's all coming out the other end," Dr. Mac explains. "It's got to be intestinal. A toxicosis of some sort. Let's get I.V.s started on everyone."

She strokes Trickster's neck, then smoothly inserts a needle into a vein. She connects the needle to a long tube that leads to the bag of clear I.V. fluid. The bags are hung from a hook on the wall of the stall.

"We have to keep his fluid level and electrolytes up. We don't want his blood pressure to drop or him to lose consciousness," Dr. Mac says. She moves down to Gertie and prepares to start her I.V.

"Wait a minute," I say suddenly. "Dr. Mac,

stop. Go back to Trickster. Look in his mouth, on the edge of his lips. He has bumps."

"Bumps?"

"I saw them earlier. He was drinking weird, too. He would stick his whole nose in the water bucket. He'd lift it to breathe, then stick it back in the water."

"What else did you notice?" She lifts Trickster's lips to look at his gums. "Think carefully."

"His stall. Jared said he had cleaned it, but when I got there, manure was everywhere. I cleaned it, but it's a mess again already. He's been having really bad diarrhea."

Dr. Mac peers in Trickster's mouth, then releases it and scratches his jaw. She looks over at Dr. Gabe. "Cantharidin."

"Couldn't be," Dr. Gabe replies, shaking his head.

"Has to be," Dr. Mac argues. "Look at these blisters."

Dr. Gabe hands Elsa's I.V. bag to Jared and looks into Trickster's mouth. He pulls a penlight out of the pocket of his coat and flashes it along Trickster's tongue.

"What is it?" I ask.

"Blister beetles," Dr. Mac says. "These horses

may have been poisoned by blister beetles in their hay. What a nightmare."

"Blister beetles? You're kidding me," Mr. Quinn says. "We've never had blister beetles before. How can you be sure?"

Dr. Mac gently holds Starfire's head and pries open his jaw. Sure enough, way back in the throat I can see the same kind of blisters I saw in Trickster's mouth, smaller but still ugly.

"That's one way to be sure," she says, releasing the horse. Starfire shakes his head and coughs. He has started to drool a bit. "We'll run some urine tests to confirm."

"What's a blister beetle?" I ask.

Dr. Mac goes back down the line and starts Gertie's I.V.

"Blister beetles live on plants like alfalfa, which is harvested for hay," she explains. "They have a chemical in their body called cantharidin. Cantharidin is not nice. It burns body tissues. And it explains all these symptoms. Trickster was keeping his whole mouth in the water bucket because it cooled the blisters on his lips. The cantharidin has irritated their stomachs, kidneys, and intestines, blistering their insides, too. That's why they are acting colicky. Their insides really, really hurt. The irritation has caused the diarrhea."

"And Gertie's seizures? Starfire's fever?" Mr. Quinn asks.

"Everything," Dr. Mac says.

Linda enters the foaling barn. She must have just come back from town. "What's going on? Why are the horses still in the pasture? Jared, you have students arriving in a few minutes."

Dr. Mac looks up. "We're pretty sure these animals have been accidentally poisoned," she quickly explains. "Have you gotten any new hay recently?"

Linda frowns. "Yeah, yesterday. It came in the nick of time. We were almost down to the barn floor." She pauses. "These horses were the first ones to get it. What's wrong? Is the hay moldy?"

Mr. Quinn dashes toward the big barn as Dr. Mac explains about the blister beetles again. Linda looks like she just came out of a horror movie.

"You mean, they were in the hay? But I didn't see any bugs. I would never feed them anything with bugs in it!"

"Of course you wouldn't," Dr. Mac says. "They

were probably chopped up, in tiny pieces. It only takes a couple of blister beetles to kill a horse. The fact that the horses are still alive proves they didn't eat very much."

Mr. Quinn steps back into the barn with a flake of hay. "Here's a sample."

Dr. Gabe stays with the horses, and the rest of us file outside to watch. Mr. Quinn puts on a pair of work gloves and scatters the hay on the ground. Dr. Mac and Linda get on their knees.

"Here, is this one?" Mr. Quinn pinches something small and black, and then drops it on the ground where Dr. Mac can see it.

"Hard to tell. Could be. Don't touch it," she warns. "It will blister your hand just like the insides of the horses. We'll analyze it."

"What can we do?" Linda asks.

"The horses in the pasture haven't eaten any of the new hay, have they?"

Jared and Linda both shake their heads.

"Good," Dr. Mac says. "Let's get some fresh hay here—from a different grower—as soon as possible. You'll need to notify whoever sold you this batch about what we found. And every stall has to be swept clean, every speck of hay removed."

"What's the antidote?" asks Mr. Quinn. "How do we treat them?"

I look at Dr. Mac.

"There is none," she says. "The best we can do is to keep their fluids up. We'll give them pain medication and antibiotics for infection."

"That's it?" Mr. Quinn asks. "That's all we can do?"

"We could transport Starfire to the equine hospital," Dr. Mac suggests. "There they can monitor his calcium, magnesium, and protein levels, which we can't do here. If his calcium gets out of whack, he could have a heart attack."

"Can't you take all of them to the hospital?" I ask. But I already know the answer. Mr. Quinn can't afford to take all the horses to the equine hospital. Starfire and the other show horses would be the ones to go. It would be way too expensive to treat unproven horses like Trickster.

It feels like something is squeezing my chest. I look up into Mr. Quinn's eyes. He looks like he feels the same way.

"I'm going to call Brenna's father," Dr. Mac says briskly. "He can take you all home."

"Wait," I say. "I can't go home—I have to stay here and help."

One of the horses in the barn whinnies.

Mr. Quinn runs his hand over his head. "Look, David, I appreciate your concern. You obviously care a lot about these horses. But I think you should go home."

"Let me stay," I plead. "The others can leave— they aren't used to being around horses, not like me. How old was I the first time Dad brought me here—five? Six? I could clean the stalls for you, get rid of the hay. Anything, just let me stay."

"David—" Dr. Mac begins.

Whump!

She's cut short by a loud crash and heavy thump from inside the foaling barn.

"J.J.!" Dr. Gabe calls from the foaling barn. "It's Starfire!"

Dr. Mac and Mr. Quinn get there before me, but not fast enough to keep me from seeing what happened.

The beautiful black stallion has collapsed in his stall. His head is stretched limply out on the straw, and his eyes are open and dull. Mr. Quinn kneels, touches the horse's leg, and turns his face away from the rest of us.

Starfire is dead.

Mr. Quinn clears his throat a few times. "David, go home. This is no place for kids. Not tonight."

Chapter Fifteen

. . . .

Midnight.

I can't sleep. No way. And it's not because of my brother's snoring. I keep thinking of Trickster. Of the other horses, too, but mostly Trickster.

He was shaking when I left. He had a high fever and wouldn't drink anything. Is he feeling better now? Is he sleeping? Awake? Is he even *alive*?

Brian jerks in his sleep and makes a sound like a surprised pig. He still smells like the popcorn in the movie theater. Maybe I could wake him up and get him to drive me back to the barn.

As if. *Turn over and go to sleep, Hutchinson.*

There's nothing else you can do. You're just a kid.

I punch my pillow and roll over so I can see out the window.

If I were going to go back to the barn, which I'm not, I'd have to do something really crazy like ride my bike there. It's got to be at least five miles. I do have a light, but that's way too far.

I should go to sleep.

But I can't.

What if Trickster is dying?

It only takes a few minutes to get dressed and leave a note for Mom so she won't freak out if she finds my bed empty. Rolling up the garage door quietly is tricky, but by midnight most people around here are fast asleep. I check the light on my bike and put on my helmet. It's time to hit the road.

• • • • • • •

All the lights are on in the foaling barn, and I can hear people talking. Their voices sound tense. I set my helmet on the seat and silently lean the bike against the wall. My stomach clenches as I run across the gravel.

What do I do now? Walk in? Pretend like I'm supposed to be here?

I peek in the door, staying in the shadows so no one can see me.

The foaling barn looks like an emergency room, crowded with veterinary supplies and oxygen tanks on every surface. Claiborne and Gus are breathing through horse oxygen masks. Elsa is lying in her stall, breathing heavily. Gertie and Trickster are wired up to heart monitors. *Heart monitors.*

Trickster's coat is shiny with sweat, and drool leaks from his mouth. His eyes blink slowly. I wish I could tell him I'm here, tell him everything is going to work out.

Suddenly, Gertie throws herself against the side of her stall. The noise startles Trickster and he flinches.

"Do something, J.J.!" Mr. Quinn says.

"I can't give her any more pain medication, Lucas," Dr. Mac says.

"I should have called the ambulance. I should have taken them all in, no matter what it cost," Mr. Quinn says as he strokes Gertie's neck.

"It wouldn't help the horses if you put yourself out of business," Dr. Mac points out.

Jared glances at his watch. "Um, Mr. Quinn, sir. Sorry, but I really have to go home. My folks said I could only stay until midnight, and it's past that. I have a Spanish test at eight o'clock."

Mr. Quinn takes a deep breath and crosses his arms over his chest. "I understand. Linda, you should go home, too. Get some sleep."

"No way," Linda protests. "I'm staying here."

"You wore yourself out cleaning up all that hay, and in a few hours, thirty-five horses are going to want breakfast. Go home and get some sleep. You're no good to me or the horses if you're exhausted."

Dr. Mac nods. "He's right, Linda. Go on. We'll manage."

"Just remember to bring us doughnuts when you come back," adds Dr. Gabe.

I hide around the side of the barn while Linda and Jared leave. This was a really dumb idea. I should go home and get back in bed. If Mom catches me, she'll ground me until I'm fifty.

"Watch out!" Dr. Gabe shouts.

I look back in the barn.

Trickster has gone totally stiff. He falls to the ground, shaking violently.

"He's seizing!" Dr. Mac says.

"Trickster!" I shout. Without thinking, I run into the foaling barn. "Trickster, no!"

I slide to the floor and brush his forelock out of his eyes. He's still shaking. "Hang in there, buddy."

"Where did you come from?" Dr. Mac asks.

I look up at her. "Can't you do anything?" I ask, my voice cracking. "He's dying!"

Mr. Quinn sits next to me. He puts one hand on Trickster's chest and the other around my shoulders. "We're doing everything we can, David. We just have to hope he's strong enough."

"He is," I say fiercely. "I know he is. Come on, Trickster. You can do it. Don't give up!"

Trickster twitches again and snorts. His nostrils flare and his eyelids flutter. I reach out my hand so he can smell me. "I'm here," I say, quieter now. "I came back for you. I won't leave until you're better. I promise."

Dr. Mac leans over with her stethoscope.

"His heart rate is slowing a bit. Good. The seizure is over. He's OK, for now."

Mr. Quinn squeezes my shoulder.

"You won't make me leave, will you, Mr. Quinn? I promise not to get in the way."

He nods once. "You can stay. We need the help." He stands up and brushes off his jeans.

"But let me call your mother. She doesn't know you're here, does she?"

"I didn't want to wake her up."

"Let me see if I can take care of it," Mr. Quinn says.

It might be that I'm tired, or maybe it's the dim light in the barn, but I swear it almost looks like he's smiling.

• • • • • • •

I don't know what Mr. Quinn said to my mom, but when he returns, he's carrying a six-pack of soda and good news.

"Your mother said you could stay," he tells me.

"Really?" I take a soda. "You're kidding. How angry is she?"

"Not as angry as you'd think. It's been a while since I talked with her. Not since your dad left, in fact. She was mostly worried about you." He pauses. "She knows this is important to you."

"David, can you get the wheelbarrow?" Dr. Mac asks. "It's getting a little too smelly in here even for my nose. Let's muck out the mess."

"Right away, Dr. Mac."

Once I've cleaned the stalls, Dr. Gabe sends me

for fresh water. After that, we bring in more supplies from Dr. Mac's van. The moon climbs into
the sky and crosses over the hill while I do all
kinds of little chores so the docs can concentrate
on the big stuff. The heart monitors beep, the
oxygen canisters hiss, and the horses cough and
whinny. Dr. Mac and Dr. Gabe take turns moni-
toring the vital signs of our patients. Mr. Quinn
watches everything. Sometimes he watches me.

Around three o'clock, Dr. Gabe goes into Mr.
Quinn's office to sleep for a few hours. He's in
charge of the clinic tomorrow—wait, that would
be today. He's going to need a clear head to deal
with the cats and dogs that are scheduled.

Mr. Quinn brings out some old horse blankets.
I wrap myself in one and sit next to Trickster.
His heart rate has slowed to fifty-five beats per
minute, much healthier. He seems to be more
comfortable. The pain medicine must be making
his stomach feel better. And his leg, too. I almost
forgot about that in all this confusion.

I pull the blanket up over my shoulders. Mr.
Quinn and Dr. Mac sit at the other end of the
foaling barn watching Claiborne and drinking
coffee. They're talking about Starfire."

"You only get a horse like that once in your life," Mr. Quinn says quietly. "He was the finest animal I ever met."

"You were a good pair," Dr. Mac says. She blows on her coffee. "He needed someone like you around to teach him. If I remember, he was a little flighty when he was young."

Mr. Quinn shakes his head with a little laugh. "And stubborn! But he learned. So did I." He looks out the window and doesn't say anything more.

It's going to be a long time before Mr. Quinn gets over this.

Trickster snorts in his sleep. I pet his muzzle.

What would Dad say if he saw me here? I wish he could. I miss him more than I want to think about—way more than I want to talk about. Some things don't fit into words.

The blanket is warm. I lean against the post to get comfortable, keeping one hand on Trickster. I can feel his pulse, strong and steady. We're going to ride. We're going to ride like the wind. I can just see us flying up the hill . . .

• • • • • •

A bird twitters overhead, and another answers from across the field. A sliver of the morning sun climbs over the hill. A rooster crows.

"What happened?" I say, waking up with a jolt. "Trickster! How's Trickster?"

"Relax," laughs Dr. Mac. "See for yourself."

I look up.

Trickster is standing over me. He bobs his head and nickers.

"Is he feeling as good as he looks?" I ask, scrambling to my feet.

Dr. Mac stands and stretches her back. "Not quite. But he made it through the night. They all did. They'll need some extra attention for a few weeks, but I think things are looking rather positive."

I grin. "You are the best veterinarian in the entire universe."

"Thanks," Dr. Mac says. "Maybe I should put that on my sign. What do you think?"

Mr. Quinn walks in the foaling barn. "I think it's time for breakfast, that's what I think. I've got a stack of pancakes in the kitchen with your name on them, J.J. Some for you, too, David. My father used to say the best way to keep good stable hands was to feed them well. Do you still like sausage?"

I can't stop grinning. "Yeah. I can't believe you remember that."

Dr. Mac studies the two of us. "I'll go ahead and wash up. Meet you at the house."

I give Trickster a few more pats, then turn to leave.

"Wait a minute, David," Mr. Quinn says, holding up his hand. His face has turned serious. Was he just acting friendly in front of Dr. Mac? "We have to talk. I've been thinking."

Uh-oh. Here it comes. Thanks for your help, but you're too young. You mess up. You cause trouble.

And I thought everything was going to work out for once.

"You and I haven't always seen eye to eye on things," he starts.

I know where this is going. I should get on my bike and head home.

"I don't have any kids of my own. Even though I watched you grow up, I could never figure you out."

"You don't have to say anything. I understand." I swallow hard. "I won't come back, don't worry."

"Wait a minute, boy. You're not listening to me! Just like your father—always jumping to conclusions, not taking the time to listen. Now sit down."

Great. Now I'm really going to get it. I sit on an overturned half-barrel.

Mr. Quinn clears his throat. "What I'm trying to say is *thank you*."

"What?"

"Thank you. Thank you for caring about these horses, Trickster and the others. I was glad you came back last night. Having you around made a big difference—to the docs, to me—and I know it helped Trickster. I think having you here helped him pull through. And you worked hard, too. Didn't complain once, did everything you were told and then some. You made a place for yourself. I'm really proud of you. I know your dad would be, too."

I have to shake my head a little to make sure I'm hearing right.

"You're not firing me?"

"Firing you? Heck, boy, I want to hire you! Anytime you get free, you bike over and I'll put you to work. I'll pay you in cash or in lessons, whichever you want. Of course, if you take the lessons, I'd prefer it if you could ride Trickster. He looks like he's going to need someone who understands mischief."

Mr. Quinn sticks out his hand to shake mine. "Do we have a deal? Let's shake and eat breakfast, then."

I reach for his hand, then pull back.

"Um, there's something I have to do first," I say. "Before any deals or pancakes."

"What's that?" Mr. Quinn asks, puzzled.

"There's a pile of manure behind your toolshed," I admit. "You don't want to know how it got there. Just let me clean it up before I do anything else. I'll feel a lot better. And then I'll eat pancakes. And all the sausage you've got."

Mr. Quinn's laugh is so loud that it wakes up the rest of the horses in the barn. They poke their heads over the stall doors to see the commotion. I start to grin again. Trickster, the chestnut with the fudge-colored forelock, bobs his head up and down, his forelock falling into his eyes.

Someday, we're going to ride.

Horse Talk

BY J.J. MACKENZIE, D.V.M.

WILD WORLD NEWS—When a horse sees you, he has only one question—*will this creature hurt me?* You might think that something so powerful and fast wouldn't be afraid of anything. You'd be wrong.

Millions of years ago, the ancestors of horses were hunted by large cats. To survive, they developed highly tuned senses and the ability to run as fast as the wind. Modern horses are rarely chased by lions, but they still run away from anything that frightens them.

If you want to be friends with a horse, you have to speak his language. That way, he'll trust you.

TO SPEAK HORSE, YOU MUST MOVE IN A WAY THAT HORSES CAN UNDERSTAND.

Horses communicate with their bodies. They sometimes use sounds like whinnies and neighs, but most of their signals are sent by the way they stand and the way they move. To speak horse, you must move in a way that horses can understand.

SAY HELLO

Let him see you. Always approach a horse from the side. Never walk up behind a horse, or approach from directly in front of him. If you startle him from behind, he might kick you. If you stand directly in front of him, he can't see you. There is a small area right in front of his face that he cannot see—a blind spot—and if you stand in the blind spot and touch him, it may startle him. Approaching from the side is friendly and safe.

Keep cool. No matter how excited you are about riding, stay calm and quiet. If you squeal, shout, or jump up and down, the horse will think you are a threat. Horses have very good memories. If you make a bad first impression, it will be hard to break. Horses like calm people.

Get to know each other. Tell the horse your name. (No, it is not dumb to talk to a horse.) Stand quietly for a minute so he can get used to you. Once he is comfortable, with his eyes and ears pointed toward you, it's time to let him smell you.

Extend your hand. He'll lower his head and sniff it. This might tickle. A horse's muzzle has tiny hairs on it that send information to his brain. If he raises his head suddenly or backs up, that means you startled him. Step back, stand quietly, and wait for him to calm down. Then try it again, more slowly this time.

Go slow. Because horses are always ready to spook or startle, moving slowly is a way of reassuring them. Some people say you should pretend you are moving underwater.

Shake hands. Once the horse has seen and smelled you, you should pet him. Always ask the horse's owner or stable manager before you touch a horse, just as you would ask the owner of a dog if it's OK to pet him. Touching is the last part of saying hello. The horse has a very strong sense of touch over his whole body. When you touch a horse in a friendly way, it is very reassuring to him.

The best way to touch a horse is to slowly bring your hand up to his jaw, his neck, or the side of his head. That way he can see you, take comfort in your slow movement, and anticipate the touch. Some horse people say it is better to gently scratch a horse than to pat him, because a pat feels aggressive. You can try both ways to see what the horse prefers.

BODY LANGUAGE

Your horse tells you all kinds of things with his body language. Pay attention to his signals so you'll know what he's feeling and what he might do next.

Ears. Horses rely on their hearing to warn them of danger. A happy, curious horse holds his ears up straight so he can hear everything around him. He may swivel his ears from side to side to figure out where different noises are coming from. When a horse is annoyed, frightened, or being aggressive, his ears will lower. If this happens, watch out. Never approach a horse whose ears are lying flat along his head. The horse is upset about something, and he may bolt or kick. Ask an adult to help you.

Head. When a horse is happy to see you, he'll hold his head in a relaxed upright position. If he feels really relaxed, he may lower his head to munch on some grass. If he raises his head suddenly, something is wrong. He has seen, heard, or smelled something that he doesn't like, and he is raising his head high to get more information about it.

Tail. The horse's tail is the world's best fly swatter. It also acts as a flag for the horse's feelings. A happy, proud horse will carry his tail high. A horse that is irritated at something will flick his tail to the side.

Legs. Always keep an eye on the legs of a horse. When he's excited, he may lift his hooves up and down, prancing like he wants to get going. If something is bothering him, a hind foot may slowly raise up off the ground a few inches, then stamp down. If he's startled or upset by something, he may kick.

Watch his leg muscles. They are so powerful and big, it's easy to see them rippling under the horse's skin. If the leg muscles tense, then the horse may be preparing to run or kick. If the legs are relaxed, your horse is relaxed, too.

Joyce Tenneson

In addition to the Vet Volunteers series, **LAURIE HALSE ANDERSON** is the author of the multiple award-winning, *New York Times* best-selling novel *Speak*, as well as *Catalyst* (an ALA Top Ten Best Book for Young Adults), *Prom*, and *Twisted* (both *New York Times* Best Sellers). She lives in northern New York with her husband and their dog.

Visit her Web site at **www.writerlady.com**.